FIREBRANDS

by Paul Yoder

A Lands of Wanderlust novel
Kingdom of Crowns series, Book 2

Visit me online for launch dates and other news at:

authorpaulyoder.com

tiktok.com/@authorpaulyoder

instagram.com/author_paul_yoder

amazon.com/stores/Paul-Yoder/author/B00D6NN4G0

goodreads.com/author/show/7096027.Paul_Yoder

ASIN : B0CKQ4MH6C

ISBN-13 : 979-8862089165

D1713699

Lands of Wanderlust Novels
by Paul Yoder

Lords of the Deep Hells Trilogy
Shadow of the Arisen
Lords of the Sands
Heart of the Maiden

Kingdom of Crowns Trilogy
The Rediron Warp
Firebrands
Seamwalker

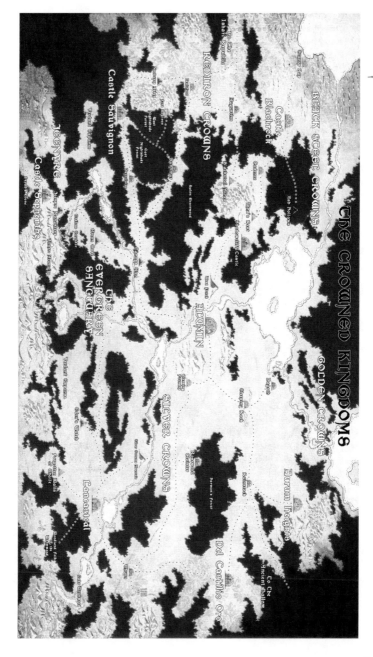

PROLOGUE

The reverend father's face had been carved off by his own hand. Where his nose and eyes should have been was now a flayed, gory wound in the shape of a crescent, seeping dark red blood down his face and neck. His lips had remained so as to allow him to recite the all-important last rites his whole life had divinely led up to.

He was naked, aside from the streams of bright, hot blood that rippled down his hairless body. Blood trickled from his mouth as he mumbled incantations in tongues that had never been spoken in all the history of Una until that night. The speech was a fledgling utterance to the realm of Wanderlust, not even the gods having knowledge of its meaning or degree of power. It was a frightful unknown to all: the divine heavens, the deep hells, and all denizens in between.

He broke from the inspired testimony, holding up blood-slicked hands before the congregation deep within the convent's chapel. The flames of the hundreds of candles surrounding him ceased to flicker, holding perfectly still as if time had stopped. The congregation froze with the flame, awaiting the father's sermon.

In a low, guttural voice, he began in the

common tongue. "Few know of thy name, fewer still know of thy ultimate glory. *Sanctus obscurus princeps* is thine epitaph by the aborted gods of never intersecting dimension. Your visage, one of enigma and frightful puissant divinity. We, thy children in this realm, are but fuel for thy inevitable quickening of flesh and embodiment of faith. We are but vessels of blood and crude matter, wholly devoted to thy fated coming."

A shiver of awe ran through him, rattling his body by the power of the procession that was about to take place. "Take us, lord god. Every turning of flesh is a step closer into this realm by thee. Umbraz, we would see thy face and behold thine true glory."

One of the congregation croaked the name *Umbraz*, others joining in the chant thereafter. The air was charged in unified purpose between the supplicants—unified in their devotion to their beloved god—unified in their insanity.

The father dug his nails into the open gash across his face, whispering feverishly, "We, the faithful of Umbraz, would see a quickening of the flesh."

The musty, dim room, lit only by the immobile flames of candlelight, darkened drastically outside of the ritual circle from which the reverend father sermonized.

The four-day-long communion of worship was coming to its conclusion. Those that remained trembled now, out of dehydration and fatigue, yes, but more so out of sheer anticipation of finally seeing the one they had performed so many difficult tasks in honor of throughout the last few years. Soon they would be deemed worthy of the title *Torchbearer*.

A sound came from within the circle, one that shook the supplicants to their core in giddy fear. Howls of the damned gurgled audibly to the surface of the ritual circle. Tortured souls morphed in and out of existence, hundreds at a time, before a great rending of flesh broke their screams, only to be replaced and overlapped by a fresh choir of howls from beyond. Those in the congregation that still stood were being assaulted with the homogenized agony of mankind.

"To this great cycle, are the faithful blessed to inherit!" the father screamed above the noise. For the first time, some in the congregation began to shake in doubt rather than in fervent worship.

"This is the fate of the *un*faithful, is it not? Is it not, Father?" a man in sullied robes shouted back, a look of innocent confusion underscoring his pathetic plight.

The father, amidst the increasing tumult in the room as the ritual quickly progressed, calmly turned his eyeless face toward the supplicant and smiled. "It is the fate of all, my son. The great Umbraz does not discriminate as the other gods do. He is the *only* fair god."

The look of horror creased into the features of

the fearful man as he realized that, despite the hefty toll of his faith over the years, not to mention the horror of the last few days, the great enigmatic god he had devoted himself to did not intend to reward him, in this life or the next.

He turned to leave the damned basement chapel, the air around him now thicker than before as though the chants of the zealots next to him were taking air from him.

His feet itched. They *burned!* As he moved a few steps closer to the chapel's doors, a fatal growth flowered within him, stopping him in his tracks amidst the cacophony of the sacred session.

His feet split in two, then again—muscle and bone warping and wrapping, spiraling slices of flesh up through his legs and into his groin. Entrails elegantly unwound before his eyes, allowing him a perfect view of his mortal demise just before his head turned clean inside out, his final scream of pain coming out as an unrecognizable squelch.

The naked father stood before the mutilated flesh, listening to the sticky squish of what was left of his poor, misguided supplicant.

"*Carry on,*" came a thought within his head. It was not his thought; it was the one that did not have a voice. Not yet, at least.

He tenderly picked up the lump of viscera that moments before was a man and carried it back to the ritual circle. He heard the fleeing steps of another worshiper trying to escape the ceremony, whimpering pathetically as he searched for a way out of the dark room. The touch of Umbraz stopped the sook in his tracks, same as the other. The father smiled as he listened for the bubbling gurgle that soon followed. Somewhere within the gory purl of each turning was a hint of his god's voice, and each syllable he reverently savored with the utmost pleasure. His god was speaking to him through others.

"Carry on," the thought came again.

In an instant, reality was torn, and a portal ripped open within the ritual circle. A dark figure, which looked carved out of glass obsidian, appeared in the center of it all. The father could feel the presence of the large object directly before him. He resisted the urge to reach out and touch the divine monument. He knew what the almighty wished of him. He had been prepared specifically for the task.

Entering the space of the other reality of his dimensional god caused his hands to flicker in and out of existence. He extended the hot, bloody pulp over to his master's welcoming embrace.

A scream roared into pitch, and the flesh grotesquely morphed partially back into the face of the fool supplicant for the briefest of moments as it merged into the obsidian totem. Fractals bloomed all around him like a halo as the flesh was engulfed.

The father wanted so badly to join the supplicant—for once to feel the embrace of the true

Father.

"Remain," a thought forcefully dominated his consciousness, causing the father to focus on his task once more. Another repetitive prompt came soon thereafter. *"Carry on."*

Guided by his master, he made his way to the next sprawl of meat. He gathered the offering and returned to the statue.

He heard no others attempting to escape. Those that remained standing in the room were true faithful —fit to become Torchbearers of Tenbriz Lux, the true name of the god Umbraz, known only to his most faithful. Some would join his circle of Torchbearers to continue their master's work; others would serve their god in a more immediate fashion that night: as fuel for his quickening. His eternal embrace did not discriminate between the faithful and the heathen.

CHAPTER 1 - UPON DEAF EARS

Warm sunlight filtered down through the grand hall's vaulted lofts, casting a lively hue on the saren knight, Reza, who stood alone at the center of the room. There were other knights present, silently watching from the balconies above, adding nothing to the proceedings other than judging glares.

Reza stood before a long table hewn from a single, massive slab of hardwood, at which sat five older women in flowing white robes with threads and adornments of gold and red woven into their stately gowns.

The sister that oversaw the proceedings sat at the center, and though all wore stern faces, the central figure seemed outright displeased with seeing Reza standing before them.

Reza grimaced, her discomfort and contempt apparent to those that filled the room. She cleared her throat and looked the center woman in the eyes. "I come here out of need. Eleemosynary has cried out for the aid of her followers. I have answered, and I seek to petition the sisterhood for their support—"

"Silence," the matriarch ordered, her voice

filling the quiet hall. "Already, you disregard our protocol. *You* do not initiate proceedings. And you should not so idly invoke Sareth's true name so lightly —you are not her speaker."

Reza clenched her fist, attempting to calm her temper but failing. "She resides in all saren, does she not? Do you alone have a monopoly on her communion?"

Gasps and whispered murmurings sounded from above in the balconies. Reza knew she was on thin ice with the High Priestess.

"Enough of this," the matriarch snapped, her distaste for the young upstart clear upon her furrowed brow. "You say you come here out of need. What is it you've come here to ask of the sisterhood?"

A hush came again to the audience hall. Reza took a steadying breath, attempting to restrain her temper. Collecting her thoughts, she laid out her case.

"I come here from the High Cliffs Monastery in Jeenyre. My matron, Lanereth, as well as a prophetess of Elendium, have had premonitions and visions of evil at work here in the Crowned Kingdoms. Lanereth is not well enough to travel, or she would have come here herself. She instead sent me to seek guidance and aid to cast a light upon the shadow of a threat taking root here in your lands. Lanereth worries that if something is not done to stunt its growth, more than just the Crowned Kingdoms will be impacted by the corruption about to spill out upon this and the neighboring regions."

The sisterhood waited patiently for Reza to conclude her speech, none showing the least bit of concern over the report.

At length, the elder broke the silence. "Lanereth has dabbled in the green lord's magic for far too long. She's likely mixing visions. We've had no such premonitions here."

"Matriarch Trensa, please," Reza replied, some softness entering her tone. "I would not have come all this way on a whim. There is a real threat within your jurisdiction—of that, I am sure."

"And to whom do you think Sareth would impart important revelations, Reza—a knight, or to her High Priestess?" Trensa quizzed in a patronizing tone. "If there is a threat, she will make it known to us."

Reza was quick to respond. "And what if she's making it known to you *right now?*"

"I've heard of your strong-willed insubordination," the older woman said after the murmurings had died down from the rest of the sisterhood. "Even the rumors did not prepare me for how disrespectful you are to the faith and the ways of your own people."

Reza's fists were clenched tight again, angry wrinkles in her otherwise youthful complexion showing a fierceness that set the others back. "I love Sareth—it's the damned church that I can't be bothered to pay respects to."

"See her out," Trensa barked, pointing a trembling finger to the door. "I don't care why you're here—I'll not have your disrespectful hide back in these hallowed halls unless Sareth herself demands I do so."

Reza's platinum hair and fair countenance seemed to glow with holy fire from the light shining upon her from the vaulted windows above, giving pause to the knights tasked to see her out. Two saren knights approached her after a moment of hesitation and ordered her to follow them to the door. Reza gave a look of utter contempt to the women at the large wood table, but she did not argue further with Trensa. It was apparent she would get nowhere with the leaders of her order.

"Reza Malay, you are hereby banished from these grounds. Do not return to West Perch," Trensa called after Reza as she departed. "May Sareth have pity upon your soul—I certainly won't."

The doors shut behind her with a resounding slam, shutting her off from her order indefinitely.

Thick raindrops pelted their travel cloak hoods as Reza stormed down the trail leading back to the city with her companion, Nomad, close behind.

In the shadows of his hood, she could see

traces of his foreign features. Far to the east he had hailed from, and hardly any in the region even knew of his people. His dark hair, olive complexion, and slanted eyes were unusual features for the Crowned Kingdoms. He stood out like a sore thumb. As such, he had kept mostly hooded during their stay in Alumin to avoid the White Cloaks that had prodded in their business more than a little over the last few weeks.

He had given her some distance upon meeting her in the foyer, instantly aware that things had not gone her way. Now that they were on the long, muddy trail home, he matched her pace and put a hand upon her shoulder to attempt to comfort her.

She shrugged his hand off roughly, in no mood for consolation.

"They threw me out just because I won't play their fucking game of theater. Damn their priggish protocol, and damn *them!*" she shouted back toward the grand keep up along the base of the mountain.

"Then why didn't you play theater with them?" Nomad murmured, just loud enough for her to hear through the pouring rain.

"Fuck you," she seethed, and immediately regretted snapping at her friend that had been through thick and thin with her.

Nomad recoiled back into his trail coat, keeping up with her agitated pace but now refusing to reply to her.

She knew none of this was Nomad's fault and that he was only there to support her. She knew that she should allow him to help her, but all that rushed through her mind just then was anger—anger toward the sisterhood, anger toward Lanereth for sending her here, anger at having just wasted their only real hope of obtaining help from anyone in all the god-forsaken Crowned Kingdoms. Her temper had gotten her thrown out of their order's temple grounds.

"I knew going there was going to be pointless," she huffed, waves of frustration boiling up the more she thought over the proceedings. "Lanereth was strict, but at least she listened to reason. Trensa and her senile council barely let me explain the situation —"

She forced herself to stop venting as it was only adding fuel to her temper. She knew nothing productive was going to come out of lobbing further blame upon the sisterhood.

She glanced at Nomad for a moment to see how he was taking the situation. He trod along the muddy trail behind her, sullen, with hood down. She had seen her companion shut down often over the last few days while awaiting her audience with the sisterhood to be approved. Things had not been pleasant between them for the last week or so with how much she had been fretting over visiting her order's headquarters. Whether she wanted to admit it or not, her order's tactics to delay the audience had gotten the best of her. Her anger had gone unchecked.

Miles on the muddy trail passed in silence save for the hard, rhythmic patter of rain pelting their hoods, numbing their thoughts, which both Reza and Nomad were thankful for. They welcomed a break from their minds.

Once they were within the city walls, the rain let up. As they neared the inn, Nomad moved up beside Reza and said in a low voice, "Might be followed."

Snapping out of her mental wanderings, Reza resisted the urge to look behind them, instead turning down a tight alley. The alley was short, and they moved quickly enough to get in position on the corner, out of sight, at the end of it.

As they waited, she wondered if it was another White Cloak that wished to interrogate them. They had almost broken down and purchased local garb after being eyed so often by officials; their attire clearly pegged them as out-of-region travelers.

Within moments, a cream-cloaked figure walked out of the alley they had just exited. Reza and Nomad stepped up to the smaller figure.

"Why are you following us?" Reza asked.

The robed figure hesitated, Reza's suddenness and tone giving her pause as Reza leaned in.

"We're going to report you to the city guard if you don't speak up," she said, pointing to a pair of guards in the highway intersection thirty yards across the street.

"I'm sorry, I'm not supposed to be here," a quiet female voice admitted, lowering her hood. "I took a risk coming to see you."

They looked upon a young woman with black, wavy, shoulder-length hair, her light blue eyes creating a striking contrast to her rich brown skin tone.

"You're a saren," Reza said, recognizing her kin's emblem on the cloak the girl wore. "You followed us from West Perch?"

"I am—I did," she stated, looking around as calmly as she could, though it was clear to Reza she was on edge. "Can we talk some place private, Miss Malay?"

Reza looked to Nomad, but his uninterested expression did little to help with a decision.

"You armed, girl?" Reza asked, gesturing for the girl to reveal what was under her cloak.

"N-no." She unbuttoned her cloak to show standard issue saren robes beneath.

"You're not a knight? A cleric or a priestess, then?" Reza asked.

"Both."

Reza gave the girl a stern look, considering the importance of the title.

"Alright. Come with us. We can talk in the inn

over supper." Reza sighed, relieved their follower was no threat to them, but displeased that her plans to take time alone the rest of the day would have to wait.

"What's your name, miss?" Nomad asked, his far eastern accent light but still noticeable.

She looked at him and answered in a quiet voice. "Kaia, Sir Nomad."

He offered his hand, taking down his hood to expose a quizzical look on his foreign features.

"We'll hear you out, but I expect an explanation on how you know who my travel companion is. I didn't drop his name to anyone at West Perch," Reza demanded, getting a nod of agreement from Kaia.

Turning to lead the two back to the inn, Reza couldn't help but seethe, "If this turns out to be a ruse, you picked the wrong day to be on my bad side."

CHAPTER 2 - CONVERGENCE OF FATES

"So what I'm hearing you say is that you're a bureaucrat?" Reza stated flatly, wiping her hands on a napkin as she finished her meal.

"No," Kaia explained, slightly exasperated at Reza's characterization of her position. "I'm on the intelligence board as a resident records analyst. I don't make motions or enact rules, I don't interact with the public; I study records. I'm just a resource for the board for the most part."

"A low-ranking bureaucrat," Nomad commented between bites, still working on the greasy chicken wings.

Kaia let out a sigh, giving up on the argument. "Well, call me what you will; that's who I am and what I do."

"You're a bit young to be on any board," Reza noted, focusing more on the conversation now that she was done with her meal. "How old are you?"

Kaia's brow furrowed slightly at the comment. "Twenty-one later this week."

"Twenty, eh?" Reza whispered as she thought out loud, following up with, "An intelligence board, you say? We didn't have anything like that at High Cliffs Monastery. What is it your department does?"

Kaia looked down in thought and attempted to sum up the day-to-day duties of her position. "Well, many things. Alumin is a large city, even for most regional capitals. Information is key to navigating the social landscape of kingdoms and constantly contested territories. The sisterhood relies upon the intelligence board to provide insight, resources, and consultation in socio-political matters, which is often needed of late with all four kingdoms on uneasy terms with each other. West Perch is a non-partied entity, which is a tricky position to be in right now when every kingdom wishes organizations to offer allegiances to them. The department I am an aid for is responsible for keeping up to speed with the political climate, knowing who we're going to offend upon any public decision, staying informed of any moves from neighboring kingdoms and groups—in general, being the eyes and ears for our order in the Crowned Kingdoms. It's not an easy position, I assure you."

Reza sat back to ruminate on the explanation.

"Spy games. I know the subject well from my time in my homeland," Nomad mused, rubbing his scruff in thought.

"We're not spies," Kaia replied.

"It seems you are not *many* things," he rebuffed.

Reza leaned back in. "Alright, so you're a bureaucratic spy—likely how you sleuthed up information on me and who I travel with. That's fine and all, but why did you feel the need to talk with us?"

"I—" she started, flustered at the assumptions and demeaning remarks piling up against her. "I'm not a sleuth. I deal with records—books! I don't do field work or interrogate people for information—"

"Then what are you doing here? Following your targets to their place of residence to ask them questions—that sounds like a sleuth to me," Reza snapped back in a hushed whisper, attempting to intimidate Kaia into lowering her voice. The rest of the tavern-goers were starting to look over at their table.

It was effective. Kaia took a steadying breath to rebase herself before answering in a much calmer tone. "Alright, maybe I am, as you say, *sleuthing* a bit, but...it feels like *I'm* the one being interrogated here."

"That's right, you are," Reza said, her voice cold and stern. She sat back in her chair, a bit more at ease with Kaia's cooperation. The other tavern patrons also went back to their conversations as the outburst seemed to de-escalate.

"You mentioned that you're also a priestess. Explain yourself," Reza demanded. "Where I come from, there's no double majoring. Do sarens at West Perch study two focuses typically? I've never heard of this."

"Not usually, no." Kaia shook her head. "I was given special permission to. I showed promise in both the healing arts and scholastics early on. My matron allowed me to pursue both for a while, and they both ended up sticking for me."

"Indeed," Reza mused, considering the humble but high-marks youth through squinted, suspicious eyes. "Now that we know a little about you, tell us"— Reza sipped from her mug of golden ale—"why have you been trailing us? What do you want?"

Kaia pinched the bridge of her nose, closing her eyes to collect herself. "You mind if I order a drink? I feel like I'm going to need it—*talking with you two*," she said, murmuring the last phrase under her breath.

"Since your birthday is later this week, I'm sure they'll let one drink slip," Reza prodded, then waved the bartender over.

Kaia frowned at the wisecrack but let the remark go after the bartender arrived and took her order. After the young saren had a mug of hot mulled wine in her hands, she proceeded. "I was at your hearing today, Reza. What you said, while brief and a bit too blunt, connected with me and some others, even if it didn't with Trensa or the council.

"I've actually done some reading on your and Nomad's exploits in the Southern Sands region over the past few months. Word has it, the Sultan of the Plainstate has leaned heavily upon your company's aid over the last few years to ward off a potentially disastrous invasion. I...would say that your actions are commendable—perhaps even heroic."

Reza shifted uncomfortably at the sudden praise. "We didn't do what we did to be commended, I assure you. We did what needed to be done, and few others were in a position or possessed the necessary skills needed to help the way we did at the time."

"Well, your actions saved countless lives, and word has trickled out from the Southern Sands. You and your company are somewhat notable, else word of your exploits wouldn't have reached so far."

Nomad, seeing Reza's momentum in the conversation slowing, stepped in. "So you know of us. Alright. What of it? Why did you seek us out?"

Earthen mug in hand, blowing steam from the hot mulled wine, Kaia started explaining between sips. "Reza's testimony before the council of the sisterhood confirmed a suspicion of mine—that there is a hidden threat working to undermine the stability of the Crowned Kingdoms."

Reza and Nomad perked up.

"You didn't get to go into much detail there in the hearing, but I would very much like to discuss the topic further with you. Perhaps we could share intel? What is this shadow of evil Lanereth told you she's seen in visions?"

Reza took a moment to decide how far she was willing to trust Kaia while the other two nursed their drinks. "Both Lanereth and Terra couldn't quite put their finger on it—they just knew something was terribly wrong, that something awful was about to happen up here in the kingdoms; something that I could possibly help prevent. I trust those two, so I came; only, it's become somewhat of an aimless, futile mission. Without the help of West Perch, I have no idea of where to look next, and that's about the extent of my connections in this region at any rate." She finished her story, taking a long draw of her ale while Kaia fidgeted with a curly lock of hair, lost in thought.

"Terra—I've heard of her as well. One of your crew? A follower of Elendium, if I recall?" Kaia mused.

"You know too much to make me feel comfortable." Reza sighed sharply after her draught.

"You know much of us, it is clear," Nomad butted in. He could feel Reza's displeasure with the day's events still sullied her mood. "It seems like you also know something about this unseen threat we're chasing. Please, elaborate on what you know."

Kaia nodded and put aside her spiced wine. "There have been a few developments in the last year or two in the Crowned Kingdoms. Seemingly small moves on the grand scale of kingdom politics, but notable for various reasons."

"What type of small moves?" Reza questioned.

"The founding of a new religion, for one. This alone isn't notable; there are new faiths born every few years: some honest, some scams, and some cults that cause more trouble than good. But this group, known colloquially as the *White Cloaks*, have sprung up out of nowhere with, at first, seemingly no connections to any organizations or ties to any other faith. Very quickly, though, they became the main religious sect of the Golden Crowns kingdom, with some representation in the Black Steel kingdom as well. Then, churches and establishments spread to the Rediron kingdom and Alumin as well— leaving essentially Silver Crowns kingdom as the last remaining territory without much representation from the cult today. It's been hard to obtain information on this company of fanatics. I don't travel, so I've just been relying on word of mouth for the most part. My intel is lacking, but the more I've looked into them, the more I'm finding that very few others have definitive answers on the basics of who this group is: how large is their body, who's the head of the sect, what are their main tenets, and what is their overall objective?"

"A mystery cult," Reza mused, tracing the rim of her mug with a finger as she considered the account. "What other small moves have you noted?"

"Valiant Synagogue, the headquarters for all followers of Elendium here in the kingdoms, has been uncooperative as of late. They've always kept mostly to themselves, rarely showing interest in outreach to the community or other religions or organizations, but since the White Cloaks showed up in the rest of the kingdom, they've all but locked the public out. All except for those within the religion, that is."

"That's Bede and Terra's faith," Reza mumbled to herself. "I know that religion better than most. I've spent a great deal of time with those two."

"I hear even Alumin city representatives have been denied audience, causing a bit of a ruckus for the city administration—all this while, for some reason, church representatives are starting to appear on the jury of cases in the city's courts. There's always trouble and drama in Alumin. It is the hub of four kingdoms, after all. There's plenty to keep officials busy, but the fact that troubles with the church started with the presence of the White Cloaks around the kingdom… I'm not sure what it means, but I wonder if some higher-ups at the Valiant Synagogue don't know something important about this new sect. The whole string of developments over the past year has been very strange. Many of the locals don't know what to make of it all, other than it smells *off*, and there's quite a bit of protest amongst the common folk. There are even murmurings amongst the upper class about these odd changes to the state's affairs."

Nomad and Reza sat back, mulling over Kaia's story. Seeing that the two had been quieted somewhat by her report, she continued.

"Followers of Elendium throughout the kingdoms last year migrated most of their congregations to Alumin. You'd be hard-pressed to find Elendium chapels filled anywhere but Alumin these days. It's almost as though the prophet has called his flock in to weather an upcoming storm. This has caused all kinds of overcrowding problems with Alumin's residents: housing and food shortages and competing laborers; the perfect circumstances for the locals here to begrudge those out of state. Things have quickly deteriorated, societally speaking, and a lot of it seems to circle back to Elendium's irregular movements. I've attempted to seek an audience with the clergy at the synagogue, but they refused my visit."

"We've seen some of these White Cloaks in Canopy Glen when we passed through—here in Alumin as well," Nomad offered. "The townsfolk did seem to give them a wide berth."

"I've seen the disastrous consequences of unwelcome oppressive religions in plenty of other regions in my time. This does seem...off to me," Reza said. She finished off her drink and added, "Do you have anything more on these White Cloaks except that they're a secretive organization? All I'm hearing are hunches."

"Well, sorry, but it seems like your Lanereth and Terra are in the same position as I am. I have a strong feeling that something is about to come of all these strange moves. The Rediron has been in disarray this whole last year; the warp sickness has crippled them. Rumors of war and invasion are constant. Both the Silver and Golden crowns have been less participatory in the Alumin council of the four kingdoms.

Something's not right, and I fear no one, even within our faith, Reza, is moving to intercept it. Everyone's just watching things go downhill. No one is interested in actually rolling up their sleeves and attempting to even understand the underlying problems at work here."

"Welcome to politics, Kaia," Reza huffed. "You're still young. You'll learn soon enough that few in power actually deserve to be there. They're often chasing some vain idea of what *they* deserve—power and repute that *should* be theirs. None up there on the council actually care about the real issues of the people—they only care that they *appear* to care. Positive public appearance is the goal with them, not actual problem-solving."

"Not all are that way while in office. I've worked with a few Alumin council members in past years," Kaia returned with a slight frown of disapproval at Reza's cynical view of their public servants.

"You're right, not all...but I would say a good majority," Reza conceded. "Perhaps they are not directly or consciously aiming to administer in such a way. Rare is it that one aims to be evil, after all. Often our actions have good motives from the outset, but slowly get tugged in all directions by the varying hooks of our flaws and base, selfish desires."

The sun had set during the course of their meal, and now the tavern began to fill up a bit more, with tenants coming back to their rooms and the bar.

"I'm rambling," Reza announced. "It's probably past your bedtime. You should get going."

Nomad attempted to soften his companion's abrupt end to their conversation. "We appreciate you following up with us. You provided us with more information than we had before—which is no small thing."

Kaia pulled her gaze off the brooding Reza to bow her head in appreciation of Nomad's remarks. "You're welcome. Though I was hoping to speak more at length with you both about the Southern Sands and perhaps even suggest collaboration on our puzzle of the Crowned Kingdoms—"

"Not interested," Reza cut in, waving her hand. "We don't need help from West Perch."

"Reza..." Nomad said, his face and tone that of a disapproving father about to correct a disobedient child.

The interaction surprised both Reza and Kaia. Reza was about to respond in kind when a man in red and gold robes entered through the front door and surveyed the room for a moment, locking gazes with the group of three. The hooded man walked up and stood before their table.

"Reza Malay?" the man queried, lowering his hood, revealing a shorn head with thin circular glasses and a humorless expression.

"And who might you be?" Reza snapped.

"I'm a faith worker at the Valiant Synagogue. Our prophet would like to talk with you at your convenience."

The table of three all gave the clergyman a look of distrust. When the cleric presented no further explanation, Reza asked, "What the hell does your prophet want to speak with me about?"

"I was asked to invite you to see him, that is all," the man replied, his voice monotone and quiet.

"If that's all the explanation you've got for me, then your job is done, get the hell out of my sight," she stated, turning back to the table to pick at her dinner plate, leaving the cleric standing there as Nomad and Kaia looked at him awkwardly.

"He would be honored for the chance to talk with you concerning Bede of Hagoth. It is his understanding that you were a close associate of hers," the cleric offered.

"What about Bede?" Reza demanded, turning back.

The man eyed Reza with some degree of contempt. "I was only told to give an invite. I know nothing about Bede, only that Prophet Yunus wishes to share information with you regarding her and her offspring."

Reza gave the man a cold, murderous glare. It was lost on him. With his message delivered, he turned to go, and none from the table tried to stop him.

There was an ominous silence at the table for a moment after the man had left the room. They all watched the silhouette of the red-robed cleric move off down the street into the night.

"How does the church know of Bede...or Terra, for that matter?" Nomad whispered once the cleric had left the inn. After digging out his pipe, stuffing, and lighting it, he added between puffs of smoke. "It doesn't smell right. What if this is some kind of trap?"

Reza shook her head, rubbing her weary eyes. "It is apparent that whoever this Yunus is has been tracking our group's actions for a while now. I need to know where this leads."

She sighed; weariness began creeping into her voice. "Besides, we're all out of leads now. Kaia just told us that the church isn't seeing anyone these days. That their prophet wishes to see me specifically is... intriguing, to say the least—wouldn't you agree?"

Nomad looked more concerned than intrigued.

Reza waved his worry off. "If this doesn't produce anything, we should head back and check up on Fin and Yozo, see if they've had luck finding Malagar."

"I'll go with you to this synagogue," Nomad offered. Kaia chipped in with, "Me too."

"Neither of you were invited," Reza replied. "And besides, who said anything about you tagging along anywhere with us?" she asked with a sideways glance at Kaia, souring the girl's features once again.

"Perhaps we could accompany you to the synagogue at least," Nomad said, throwing a line to Kaia, who seemed more saddened than perturbed by Reza's rebuff.

"I suppose." Reza rubbed her brow. The excess amount of ale and lack of water was catching up to her. "Though, before we plan anything further, or before any other strangers approach me, I'm going to get some sleep. We'll pick this up tomorrow. Today just needs to *end*."

Nomad and Kaia shared a look of concern as Reza abruptly got up from the table and left upstairs to her room.

"Is she always like this?" Kaia asked, not quite sure how protective Nomad was of his travel companion.

"Lately, more than ever," he admitted, a subtle sadness lining his tone as he reflected on his companion's dark mood.

CHAPTER 3 - FIRST IMPRESSIONS

The early morning sunrise was Kaia's only source of warmth on the empty street outside of the inn where Reza and Nomad were staying. She stood shivering alone as she waited for the pair to emerge.

Reza came out first, her brow still furrowed as it had been most of the previous day. Nomad was close behind. His demeanor brightened when he saw Kaia across the way, and he waved to her as they crossed the street to exchange "g'mornings."

"You'll freeze out here dressed in naught but a robe," Nomad gruffed, taking off his cloak and draping it around her. "You're the local among us; don't you have anything more fitting for a cold early morning?"

Teeth chattering, she answered, "I r-rarely leave the g-grounds, or the study for that matter. I'm never out this e-early."

Nomad rubbed some warmth into her along her shoulders and back, seeing how frozen the girl had gotten waiting for them.

"Should have just waited for us inside!" he offered.

"It was l-locked when I got here," she shivered.

Reza's frown did not let up as she waited for the pleasantries to pass between the two.

"Well, better not keep the prophet waiting," Nomad said, seeing Reza glaring at them.

The three started off in the cold misty morning with Kaia leading the way. The sound of chattering teeth slowly died off as they made their way to the capital's central avenue.

"I'm assuming that monstrosity of a building is the synagogue we're looking for?" Reza grumbled in a morning voice.

The three looked up to the white-spired temple a few streets away, towering over the neighboring establishments on the outskirts of its grounds. Though the building's architecture was from a bygone age, it still looked well-kept and tended to.

"Yes, that is Elendium's house of worship. Their prophet resides there," Kaia said, her breath pouring frosted smoke with each syllable.

"You know what you're going to say to this prophet?" Nomad asked, looking to Reza.

"No idea," she admitted. "I just want to know what he wants with Terra."

"The mention of Bede and her kin...that was indeed concerning." Nomad thought back on the strange invitation from the cleric the evening prior.

"Their faith is fallen, as far as I'm concerned. They've been on a path separate from their god for a while now. My time with Bede gave me many insights into their religion. The gospel and their order have been fracturing over the last few generations. I worry they would have censured Bede had she lived through the events in Brigganden if she ever returned and reported to her order."

Reza's eyes were locked on the white spires looming before them, the chill morning tightening its grasp as the sun hid behind clouds. "I worry what they'll do to Terra if they come to learn of her divine connection to Elendium. Her order put an end to female prophets during Bede's life. With Terra having Elendium's favor...I suspect the church would not like that development."

"We'll accompany you as far as they allow us," Nomad offered, putting a supportive hand on her shoulder. "You keep on your toes in there," he whispered to her.

The three approached the closed gates of the synagogue grounds and waited. They were just about to start snooping around the plot's perimeter when the same cleric that visited them the night before opened the foyer door and came toward them to unlock the gate.

"Welcome," the man greeted as he led them to the expansive building's entrance.

"Once inside, you are expected to use a reverent tone. Any blasphemy, crude language, or loud voices will not be tolerated, and you will be escorted out of the building. Please respect our house of worship," the man explained, as though he had given the same speech thousands of times before.

"Reza." The man turned to address her as they passed through the threshold into the foyer. "Your companions are welcome to wait for you here in the foyer or the chapel to our left, but the prophet wishes to visit with you alone."

Nomad rubbed Reza's shoulder in support once before she nodded her agreement to the terms.

"Is he awake? Am I able to meet with him now?" she asked.

"His holiness is often awake in the early hours these days. I've already sent word of your arrival. Jonas should be returning soon to send for us."

They waited there in silence, the spacious, empty anteroom giving the three guests an uneasiness that the cleric waiting with them willfully ignored.

A few minutes passed by before an older clergyman shuffled in from deep inside the synagogue's many corridors and announced, "His Holiness will see you now, Miss Malay."

"Jonas, will you stay with our other two guests while they wait for their companion's return?"

"Certainly," Jonas replied.

Without another word, the cleric walked briskly into the twisting corridors, making Reza hurry to catch up.

The halls were all white and gold, paintings of saints of the faith hanging like shrines throughout the building, warm candlelight turning the pure white walls a creamy hue. Marble stonework framed each doorway, leaving Reza with the feeling that whoever had been involved with the making of the synagogue were master craftsmen in their respective trades.

A golden banister led them up a sweeping stairwell, guiding them up two flights. The whole ascent, Reza couldn't help but stare fixedly at the white crystal chandelier that hung at the center of the tall domed room. It was of an otherworldly fashion and well over fifteen feet long from silver chain to crystal tip. If she hadn't so much distaste for the religion itself, she could easily see herself appreciating the beauty of it all.

The hall at the top of the stairs was deathly quiet, and the candle and window light was more sparse. After an uneasy walk down two more halls, they came to a grand door, where the cleric stopped.

"Prophet Yunus, the saren knight, Reza Malay, is here," the cleric announced at the door.

"Come," an authoritative voice ordered from within.

The cleric opened the door. Reza had seen opulent offices in her day, but the prophet's study, even by a king or sultan's standards, was impressively fitted. White wood furniture with golden inlays filled some of the room; there was a study, a small library of ancient holy texts, and a few seats for work and visiting.

Behind the center desk sat a man well into his middle ages, if not early in his silver years. The grand window behind him at first blinded her, but as the man stood and began to speak, her eyes adjusted.

"Reza Malay. I've heard much of your recent victories in the Southern Sands region. By all accounts, without you, the southern territories would still be struggling with Sha'oul's raiders."

Reza looked to the door that had closed behind her, then eyed the religious man.

"Forgive me, I haven't introduced myself," he said. "Alister Yunus, a prophet and president of this synagogue and humble servant of Elendium."

He offered his hand to Reza, and after a brief hesitation, she obliged.

"Have a seat, please." He gestured to the chair across the desk before taking a seat himself.

"It seems you already know my name and those of my associates, along with my work history," she said as she finally took a seat in the chair across from him. "You called me here to ask me about Bede, but before you ask me anything about her, I want to know why you care about her and her kin."

"Fair enough." The prophet nodded, easing into his seat. "I suppose there is no harm in disclosing my interest in the field cleric Bede and her offspring. It is my understanding that she shepherded a small flock of followers of our faith in the Plainstate for years, even against the council of the church. We found it of little significance at the time, and she was, at length, forgotten. There are not many followers of Elendium in the Southern Sands, after all. We disapproved of her representing the faith down there but made no move to stop it either."

"Why did you disapprove of her leadership?" Reza questioned.

"She was never appointed to do so. She simply took it upon herself to represent our faith in that region. Our faith is one of order, Miss Malay. This distinction is important to us—even if it is not in your faith."

"Don't lecture me on what's important in my own faith," Reza snapped.

Yunus held up his hands. "To the point, we learned of her passing some seasons ago. But with the news of her death also came news of the threat you, your company, and the combined forces of the Southern Sands region were facing at the time. By the time we had prepared aid to send your way, the conflict was over, and the war had been halted before it had gathered any steam, thankfully."

"I don't need a history lesson. I was there for it all. Cut to the chase," Reza said, crossing her legs. She was growing tired of the prophet's casual tone. It perturbed her that a man so high in her old friend's faith, who had all but snubbed Bede's life work, only now seemed interested.

The older man did not look pleased with Reza's tone, but he did as she asked and returned to the subject. "Bede had offspring. None of particular note, save for one. A Terra of Hagoth. Terra was said to have taken part in the battle of the Red Gate. She was said to possess power from Elendium."

"Yes, she did. I saw his holy might channel through her," Reza agreed.

The robed old man steepled his fingers, for the first time in their conversation taking his eyes off his guest to ponder over the account. Reza did not press the point, allowing the prophet to think through what she had just told him. She hoped he would come to terms with his god having favor in Bede's family line. She had long thought Bede and her kin deserved vindication for her and Terra's contributions to their faith.

Looking back to Reza, he asked, "What became of Terra after that?"

She couldn't quite place it, but something had changed in the prophet's countenance—something that warned her to be on guard.

"She...was shot in the heart with a crossbow bolt by a soldier in Brigganden," Reza confessed, closely observing the man's reaction to the news.

"Did she die?" he asked. His compassion seemed genuine.

"It pierced her heart," Reza reiterated.

"My sincere condolences. As I understand from the reports, she numbered among your company." Yunus spoke softly, giving the announcement a moment of silence out of reverence. "Oddly enough, there have been rumors that she lives," Prophet Yunus explained, easing into the account of hearsay.

"Who says that?" Reza asked, a cautious dread settling in her stomach.

"The church's influence is recognized far and wide. Brigganden officials sent communications with us over the matter after the war in the region had subsided," he said. Reza caught a glimpse of a keen, calculating look a moment before he softened on the topic. "It's only a rumor. We haven't been able to validate the news. Honestly, that is the main reason I was interested in speaking with you. You, more than anyone, might be able to confirm or deny those claims."

Reza eyed the man, trying to decide if she was willing to lie to the prophet of a very influential, and powerful, religion.

At length, she sighed and looked down at her lap. "I wish I *could* confirm that she's alive and well."

Prophet Yunus studied Reza, waiting to see if she had more to say on the matter. He soon realized that was the extent of what he'd get out of her without further probing.

"Yes, as do all her loved ones, I'm sure," he offered, already deep in thought, steepling his fingers once more.

A knock came at the door, dispelling the moment.

"Come," the prophet called.

A female faith worker with a thin veil over her face entered, head bowed, and shuffled to his deskside.

"President Yunus, you wanted the report from Rosewood as soon as it arrived," the woman mumbled. She gingerly placed the file of papers on the prophet's desk before bowing and exiting as quickly as she had come.

The prophet's sharp eyes met Reza's for a moment. She could feel tension there briefly before he played off the interruption. "Well, if you can't confirm Terra's whereabouts, then I suppose I cannot either. Perhaps what was reported to me was merely a case of mistaken identity."

Yunus got up and made his way to the door, Reza following suit. "If you do ever come across Miss Terra again, please let her know that I wish to speak with her. A talent and saint such as her should not be wandering. She has a home here, with her brothers and sisters in the faith."

Reza nodded and begrudgingly accepted the

old man's extended hand. He opened the door at length. Reza couldn't help but eye him one last time, searching for some hidden motive of the meeting. She gave up the search as the cleric that had guided her there approached to take her back to the foyer.

When she was reunited with Nomad and Kaia, it was clear they were more than ready to leave the premises. None spoke, not even the cleric seeing them to the streetside gates as they left the towering synagogue.

"Well, that was unsettling," Reza admitted as they strolled back to the inn, a block of city now between them and the church.

"It was indeed." Kaia looked back to make sure none from the synagogue had followed after them. "Something has changed there since last I visited a few years ago."

"How so?" Nomad asked.

"They kept an eye on us the whole time. And we were the only ones there. Where are their parishioners? Where are the visitors curious about the faith? There was a strange air about the place." Giving the experience some more thought, Kaia continued. "I mean, with all the influx of members for surrounding nation-states, why isn't their headquarters packed?"

The question lingered with the group.

"What about you, Reza?" Nomad asked.

"Something didn't feel right about the whole thing. I had never been to this synagogue before, but it was unusually empty for such a large building. Kaia is right. There should have been at least more synagogue workers than there were at the very least."

"What did they want with Bede or Terra?" Nomad asked.

Reza looked to Nomad, then to Kaia, and remained silent.

This was not lost on Kaia. "I...suppose I understand if you wish to discuss sensitive information without me."

They walked in silence for a few awkward moments before Reza asked, "Kaia. What do you know of a place called Rosewood?"

Kaia tilted her head, looking into the sky as if the answer were somewhere in the gray clouds above. "I...think that's a mission somewhere to the east. I could be wrong. I could check for you."

"See to it," Reza agreed. "Meet us back at the inn this afternoon?"

Kaia smiled. "I can do that."

Thunder cracked across the sky as dark storm clouds began to roll in from the north.

"Better be quick about it," Nomad suggested. He patted Kaia on the back, prompting her to skip off back to West Perch's library, leaving Reza and him alone again on the street.

They watched the young girl rush off before Reza whispered to her old friend, "I get the feeling that we're about to get wrapped up in something bigger than what we signed up for."

Further down the street, two white-robed cultists began to raise their voices in the midst of a holy sermon. The crowd around them gave them space, attempting to avoid the attention of either preacher.

Normally, Reza and Nomad would have expected to see some pushback from the locals going about their day in a market district. Street preachers rarely went un-harassed for long in the societies they had lived in. But the people seemed almost afraid of the two White Cloak proselytizers.

"I'd have to agree," Nomad sighed, putting an arm around her and guiding her through a side street instead of passing the two White Cloaks. They hurried back to the inn as it started to sprinkle.

CHAPTER 4 - A NEW HEADING

It had poured for most of the afternoon. By evening, the inn was packed full of tenants that had been forced to return to shelter and the warmth of the toasty hearth in the dining room.

Nomad had come down from their room just in time to snag a window seat in an alcove across from the sitting room. He had been nursing a cup of tea when Reza finally came down after her nap.

He patted the spot next to him on the bench next to the bubbled window. A light rain lingered, pattering against the side of the building with the occasional rumble of thunder in the distance.

"Well rested?" he asked with a warm smile, knowing that she had desperately needed the time to unwind upstairs.

"Sure," she mumbled, looking around for a barmaid.

"Might be a while till someone comes by for your order. What would you like me to get you?"

She held her hand up to stop him and came to sit next to him. A gentle bump with her hip prompted him to scoot over to make room for her. The two settled in the cozy nook.

"What's this?" she asked, picking up the tall pitcher.

"Closest to red tea as I could get." He smiled. The drink only resembled red tea in color.

She lifted the small lid and sniffed. "Fruit?"

"Guess that's what red tea is here," he said with a shrug.

The first floor of the inn was busier that evening than they had seen it since their arrival two weeks earlier. They were not sure when, or if, Kaia planned to return to talk with them about the Rosewood lead, but Nomad had figured the common area would be good as any to have a chat with the girl. With all the noise in the inn, there was little chance of eavesdroppers.

"What did the prophet have to say to you?" Nomad asked, leaning in to make sure Reza could hear him.

Reza's already tense demeanor spoiled somewhat at the mention of the meeting she had attended the night before. She sighed and poured a cup of tea for herself.

"He wanted to know details about Bede and Terra," she started, taking a sip. "Mostly about Terra. He knows about Bede's death. He heard rumors about Terra's near-fatal shooting in Brigganden, heard that she might still be alive, but wanted confirmation of it from me."

"Did you give him confirmation?" Nomad asked.

"No. A creep like that can't stay far enough away from Terra. Who knows what he'd do with that information."

"That's precisely what I wanted to speculate about with you." Nomad's finger idly traced the rim of the mug as he thought over the church's interest in their friends. "We need to know if they're a threat to Terra. How likely are they to hunt her down, and what would they do with her once she's found?"

Reza sat looking off into the crowded gathering room. Things were starting to settle a bit more; patrons were retiring to their rooms now that most had finished with lunch. There was still plenty of bustle to force her and Nomad close to hear over the din.

"Reza," Nomad prompted, seeing her drift off in thought. "I don't know this religion well. You've spent much more time with followers of Elendium than I. What could they possibly want from Terra?"

"I don't know," she snapped, more frustrated with her lack of understanding than her companion's pestering.

"Damn it, Reza," Nomad huffed, bringing a fist down on the table hard enough that a few passersby glanced at the couple. "You've clammed up since we arrived here. I know this trip has been hard on you; you were given hardly any direction or guidance by

Lanereth as to why she wanted you in the Crowned Kingdoms in the first place, but don't take it out on the only friend that chose to be by your side."

Nomad could tell her feathers had been ruffled, but she held her tongue and looked away.

She knew he was right. She had been on pins and needles since arriving in Alumin. The sisterhood had toyed with her, delaying her chance to address them by leveraging convoluted protocol and causing her to squander precious time here instead of back on the road. For all they knew, their friends Fin, Yozo, and Malagar could very well be in trouble in the Rediron kingdom. The waiting had made her itchy and on edge day after day. Nomad had taken the brunt of her frustrations. A punishment she knew he did not deserve.

She was about to address his complaint when the inn's front door opened, and a very wet Kaia walked in, looking thoroughly cold and miserable.

"Here," Nomad called out, grabbing her attention.

She made her way over to them and took a thin book from the folds of Nomad's borrowed wet cloak, placing it on the table.

"P-page n-nine," she shivered, hanging the cloak to dry on the coat rack as she went to warm herself by the hearth.

Reza flipped to page nine, opening to a spread

of maps. "Is this the Silver Crowns kingdom?" She looked through all the topographical drawings and recognized some of the labeled landmarks on paper that looked to be newly inked.

"It's a map of the contested regions between the Golden and Silver Crowns—territory border markings and such. It's the most up-to-date print I could find of the area I was looking into. See there?" Kaia's ice-cold finger pointed to a stretch of woods along the border of the two kingdoms. "I thought Rosewood sounded familiar. You wanted to know what Rosewood was, or where it was? Well, it's here."

"Where is that? How far from Alumin is it by foot?" Reza asked, making room for Kaia to have a seat with them on the crowded alcove bench.

Kaia scooted in at the end of the bench. "That's between the Golden and Silver Crowns territories to the east. Probably only a few days' walk by the looks of it. See? Here's the edge of the capital's borders, and there's the Glensing Foundry town not but a day's journey once you get past the Alumin city walls."

"You know anything about this cloister?" Reza asked. "What is it, an abbey?"

Kaia rubbed herself warm, teeth still chattering slightly. "Possibly. I don't know much about that area. I did ask a colleague about it. They thought it was some sort of chapel estate belonging to the followers of Elendium."

Reza nibbled at her lips as she looked over

the map. "Nomad," she murmured after some contemplation.

Nomad gave her his attention.

"Ah, never mind. It's such a little hunch to go off of." Reza waved away pulling the Rosewood thread. "We're still early for our rendezvous with Fin and Yozo back in Canopy Glen, but might as well pack up, head out, and wait for them there. I think we're all settled here."

Nomad sipped his tea as he mulled over her decision. After pouring Kaia the last of the pitcher, he finally waved a waitress over now that the joint had begun to clear out.

"Something hot for the girl," he ordered and gave a smile to Kaia, who still shivered sporadically.

"Steamed sweet bean buns sound good?" the waitress asked, to which Nomad and Kaia both readily agreed. Reza was still off in her own thoughts, hardly aware of the exchange.

"A visit to Rosewood will have to wait for another day, I suppose," she mused, still looking over the chapel symbol on the map.

"Good choice," the waitress replied. At first, they were not sure if she was simply agreeing with their order. "...To hold off on visiting Rosewood, that is."

"Why do you say that?" Reza asked.

"Strange happenings there. Some reports of missing persons, and since the church owns the land, not much has been done from either the Goldens or Silvers," the serving woman explained as she cleared the table somewhat. "Probably going to come to a head at some point, but till then, well, just ain't a smart place to plan a day trip to."

"Rosewood," Kaia mumbled after the waitress had left them, looking at the spot on the map upon which Reza had been fixated.

"Something doesn't feel right about that place." Reza looked to Nomad, who shared her distrust of the mysterious religious site.

"We do technically have a few weeks till we were going to meet back up with Fin and Yozo. Seems Rosewood is only a few days' journey from here," Nomad offered, smiling as the waitress hurried back to them with a steaming pile of plump, white buns. "If your gut is pointing you in a direction, why not go with it?"

"There ya go, dears. Anything else I can do for you?" the waitress asked as she placed a new pitcher of tea out and took the empty one.

"That's all. Thanks," Nomad answered for the group. He sampled the first bun, and Kaia joined him.

"We should have been ordering these our whole stay," he lamented, offering one to Reza, who distractedly accepted.

"Nomad, I'm serious," she said. "Should we take the time to investigate Rosewood? It sounds shady, sure, but I'm not sure it's connected with Malagar, Terra, or the threat Lanereth spoke of."

"And we won't know that it's not until we look into it ourselves," Nomad replied. "I'm with you whether you decide to investigate Rosewood or head back to Canopy Glen; but knowing you, I suggest we make a quick stop there and clear Rosewood off your mind to put it to rest. We've got the time to do so, after all."

Reza mulled over her companions' counsel, picking at the bun as she studied the map. Her eyebrows raised in approval as she nibbled at the sweet bean filling.

"Perhaps we can even return to Canopy Glen through the Silver Crowns countryside on the way back—allow us to see more of the kingdoms," Nomad suggested, pointing to the highway that led down and around back to Canopy Glen.

Kaia jumped in. "Silver Crown's countryside isn't the easiest to navigate. I've been that way before. The trails are quite scenic and not well-marked. You'd need some good maps. And haltia aren't the most welcoming folk, especially to outsiders. They tolerate visitors from other kingdoms, but with you two being from the Southern Sands, there may be inquiries."

Reza still looked unsure about the whole thing. She closed her eyes and soothed her temples rather than weigh in on her present company's comments.

"You know of the haltia, yes? They're not like

humans, sarens, or praven. They're—"

"Yes, I've seen haltia before," Reza interrupted.

"Your road would be much smoother if I came along with you."

Reza issued a heavy sigh. Since meeting the girl, she'd been worried about snagging another travel companion.

"Kaia...I have many concerns and objections to picking up another tagalong. I'm not going to belabor you with them all. My answer is no. Thanks for your help so far—but no."

"Belabor *me* with them then," Nomad cut in.

She could tell he was not joking; all lightheartedness had dissipated. She didn't like when he looked at her like that. For all his patience, he had a stubborn side to him that rivaled even her own iron will.

"Nomad..." she started, thinking to argue with him on the matter, but reconsidered as his determined stare halted her in her tracks.

She hadn't thought much of it until that moment, but she could see that he had taken a liking to the quiet young saren. She would need a good reason to turn the girl away if she was to have the final say on the matter.

Nomad beat her to the mark. "I was once a *tagalong* in your company, Reza—so was Jadu, Zaren, Arie, and plenty others. Kaia has given us no reason to distrust her thus far. In fact, she's been one of the only helpful, friendly contacts that we've come across since James in Canopy Glen. If she's willing to travel with us for a time and act as a local guide, why turn her down?"

Reza glared at Nomad, seeing that he was willing to make the point personal by bringing all their friends into this decision. She turned to Kaia. "You're able to just take off from the order to wander the countryside with some strangers you've read about from region reports? You sure the sisterhood wouldn't expel you from West Perch on the spot if they knew you were traveling with me?"

Though Reza was clearly scoffing at the notion, Kaia took the question seriously. "I wouldn't tell them I'm traveling with you, obviously. Aside from that, it isn't irregular to travel the kingdoms to gather intel firsthand. A few on my board engage in fieldwork regularly enough. Silver Crowns kingdom is a good destination for me to record a dossier of. We've not had fresh news from there for a year or two. With my credentials, it'd make the trip much smoother for you two."

Nomad smirked slightly at the response. Reza, on the other hand, was not entertained.

"Why do you want to attach yourself to us so badly?" she asked bluntly.

Nomad looked to his friend and lover. He knew her on a more personal level than any other in recent years. He knew her main concern had just surfaced and that whatever Kaia's answer was to the question would likely determine her future with them.

"I've read about you, Reza, for a good while now. You...aren't like any other saren I've met at West Perch. You've been out there," she said in a reverent tone, looking out past them through the thick window to the cloudy horizon. "You've done more than most notable sarens I've read about in the old history tomes."

Both Reza's and Nomad's features softened as they listened to the dreamy youth. It was clear that she thought a lot of Reza, even with how rude the travel-frayed saren had been to her.

"I don't want to end up just a record pusher at West Perch, always bending to the sisterhood's senile, strict hand. It's musty in there—cold, lifeless. I'm young, I know, but isn't youth meant for pushing yourself, stepping over boundaries—adventure? I don't want any regrets about how I choose to live. I'm already starting to feel that itching feeling of wasting time on the board. Perhaps it's selfish, but I want to join you to break things up in my life a bit, I guess."

Nomad grabbed a bun. Reza could tell that he knew the debate had been settled. It was the same *itching feeling* of wasting time in a stringent matriarchal system that led her to ship out on her own path. She understood the girl perfectly in that sense.

"Sure, fine," she gave in, putting her hands up in defeat. "Come with us if you wish—but we're not going to slow down for you. You keep up with our pace, and Sareth help you if you turn out to be an annoyance."

"The most benign personality would annoy you, Reza. Ease up on her," Nomad remarked between mouthfuls.

Kaia ignored the threats, hardly able to hide her satisfied smile.

Reza stared blankly at the jubilant youth and returned to rubbing her temples, grumbling, "Gods, I'm going to need a long, hot bath before we hit the trail again."

"That's...actually a great idea," Nomad agreed. He patted both women heartily on the shoulders, sealing the arrangement and welcoming their new companion.

It was rare that Nomad saw Reza indulge in pleasures and vices, but while Kaia spent the following days prepping for their trip to Rosewood, Reza had taken off for the day and did not return to the inn until well after dark.

She had not said a word upon entering the room. Nomad could see instantly that she was not her usual, high-strung, intense self. Her clothes smelled of smoke, a particular odor similar to strains of depressants he had known throughout the years.

Her eyes were deadpan, showing no desire to engage with him on any subject. She fumbled with her clothes, stripping off her garments, and flopped in their shared bed.

He considered her arrival for a moment, thinking to snatch a pipe from his pack, seeing that the room now already smelled of smoke. He lit up in the dim, candlelit room to think over his dear friend's rough patch of late.

It was clear she felt aimless. *This is her weakness*, Nomad thought. Without something at which to direct her intensity, she unraveled. He sardonically chuckled softly to himself at the irony of her predicament. She only ever seemed at peace when she was embroiled in conflict. It simplified all else in her life—made decisions come easy to her.

He smoked a few bowls of his ko mixture, ruminating on their stay in Alumin over the last few weeks. He hoped that they would carry no lasting damage to their relationship upon their departure.

Kaia had been an interesting development—a trivial but welcomed one for his part. Both he and Reza needed a change in their routine, even if Reza would never admit to it. The girl would provide just that; she seemed goodhearted and pleasant enough to not disrupt their day-to-day too much.

He thought little of the Rosewood lead, but the idea of waiting weeks for Fin and Yozo to return in

Canopy Glen with an overly irritable Reza worried him more than a little. This *wolf* needed a target to hunt—legitimate or not. Without it, she was going to tear anyone around her to shreds.

The room's candle went out, leaving him burning embers a little longer into the night, watching the mess of a woman who lay passed out and intoxicated on their bed. For both of their sakes, he hoped she soon found some tangible threat to fight against. Without an enemy, she would be condemned to confront an even more devastating foe—herself.

CHAPTER 5 - THE GLOOMY ROAD

The damp grassy plains had proven miserable to traverse, even with the patchy cobblestone roads that afforded them a clear direction to the Rosewood crossing. After passing through Glensing, they had headed west. The rain cast a dour mood upon the newly established travel group the entire way.

The weather had forced them to stop at Glensing to acquire Kaia some road-appropriate attire, a fact that had Reza fuming even a day later. With a constant drizzle throughout the rest of the traveling day, they trudged steadily eastward along the patchy cobblestone until they reached the crossroads that split off to Lancasteal, Thurn, and northward to what they all assumed led to Rosewood.

"Silver Streams," Nomad read aloud from the worn signpost, looking south to a mountain far in the distance, almost out of sight.

"Thurn, to the east," he continued, eyes locked on the sign. He pointed toward a valley with endless miles of plains and tree lines on both sides.

"And no sign for that trail that leads north," Reza concluded, not interested in the other paths in the least. Her gaze was fixed upon the dark woods looming miles to the north of them.

"Think that's where Rosewood lies?" Nomad asked Kaia.

Happy to be included, she answered, "Don't know for sure, but according to the map, that dirt road should be the path to it."

Reza scowled as low-hanging rain clouds lazily drifted over the already unwelcoming tree line, promising the three no confirmation of what lay a few miles up the muddy trail.

"What do you think, Nomad?" Reza took her eyes off the miserable trail to address the quiet man who was fixated on something in the opposite direction.

"A caravan," he announced, nodding to a small group of horses and a wagon. The group of ten trotted slowly up along the road toward them. "Want to wait for them? We could chat them up about Rosewood."

Reza tossed her trail pack beside the post and sighed. "Might as well."

Minutes passed in silence as the three watched the slow-moving caravan pass over the dreary stretch of fields between them.

"Ho there," the lead rider called out, leisurely trotting up to the three.

"G'day," Nomad returned with a wave. "How has the road treated your company this day?"

"Fair enough, and you?" the man replied, frisking his spruce mustache and pointed chin hairs.

"Other than the drab weather, not too bad." Nomad shifted his weight. "You travel with a sizable crew. Headed to Alumin by chance? Trade or leisure?"

The horseman caught Nomad's prod and nodded. "Not headed to Alumin—Glensing, rather. Transporting exports from Silver Streams."

Nomad rubbed his chin thoughtfully. "Let me guess...silver?"

The man genuinely chuckled. "We've got a smart one here." This merited a smile from Kaia and a glance from Reza.

"And you, sir?" the horseman asked.

"Just travelers passing through. Actually, we had a mind to visit Rosewood. You know if that trail northward leads there? There's no signpost for it, but our map suggests this is the road we've been looking for."

The man's mood changed instantly. He shook his head. "You'd not want to go there, especially with two lovely ladies. Beggin' your pardon, misses, but those grounds belong to the church. Was a small, off-the-trail nunnery years back. Of late, who's to say, but there's been a foul air about the place."

"Foul air?"

"Mmm, yes. Unsavory folk been known to travel there. Zealots, for lack of a better word. White Cloaks most calls 'em. Migrated from the western kingdoms and Alumin, they say. There have been a few accounts of missing persons in this area. Silvers know to stay away. It's contested territory anyways, been dangerous to venture or hunt there for years with the Golds occasionally patrolling that land, but since the church started sending more faith members there, it's been nothing but trouble."

"Why hasn't the Silver Crowns' military done anything to investigate it?" Reza cut in.

The man smirked. "You lot really must be fresh to the Silver Crowns. Tensions between the kingdoms have run high over the last few years—with Alumin as well. The church is quite a large organization and has sway in many places. Silver legislators seem to think it's best not to test the church on the matter. It ain't exactly clearly within Silver's borders, after all. Too little gain for too high a risk and all. Besides, there's nothing up there but Harmon's Forest, and there's better game in the forests south of there anyways. You'll only find strange men in robes and trouble up that road."

The caravan slowly trickled in, crowding the crossroads. Calling commands back down the line, the horseman turned to the three once more, his horse starting to trot in place. "I'd not venture there if I were you. Nothing but trouble, believe me. Try Thurn up the road. Best wine in the kingdoms."

With a whistle and a slap of reins along the

horse's neck, the man trotted ahead of the caravan, leading them off to the west to Glensing. Soon, the three were alone at the drizzling crossroads once more to contemplate the update.

The clouds that drifted across the northern tree line seemed darker now. All three started up the trail for some time before Reza broke the eerie silence. "Kaia, this would be where we part ways."

"Whoa, wait a second—" Kaia started.

"I don't care how willing you are to jump into something like this. I'm not going to have you slow us down, give us away, or die while in our care."

Nomad stepped in. "Let's back up," he said, looking to Reza first. "You're wanting to still head to that place after the warning that tradesman gave us?"

"Yes, of course." Seeing his concern, she continued. "We felt there wasn't something right with the church from the start. Hell, even before we came to the kingdoms. You remember in Brigganden? They claimed to be associated with the church. They wore white robes as well. We just thought of them as some wayward sect of Elendium, but what if they actually were acting under the direction of the prophet here in the kingdoms? What if this offshoot sect, these *White Cloaks*, are actually represented by the church of Elendium? That would clearly explain why Bede and Terra had such issue with their faith and why the prophet wants to find Terra now."

Nomad was left speechless, the deluge of

accusations and speculation giving him pause. Reza pressed her theory. "If Rosewood is important enough to be a priority subject for the prophet, then it's worth looking into. This could be the shrouded threat Lanereth had visions of. Surely it would be a related concern for Terra and may be why she's having similar premonitions regarding the dissension within her faith."

"That would be huge if it were true. The sisterhood would need to know about it," Kaia said.

"I don't give a fuck what the sisterhood knows or doesn't know. All they'll do is sit at their table and reject any sense that comes their way," Reza cursed, passions instantly flaring at the mention of the leaders of her faith.

"If Rosewood is somehow associated with this White Cloak cult, then perhaps investigation would be merited," Nomad reasoned. "If it turns out to be true, then I agree with Reza. From what we've heard and experienced of this cult, they're dangerous, Kaia. It's no place for a young tenderfoot like yourself. We'd need to infiltrate those grounds alone. We surely won't be walking up to the door on this one."

Kaia frowned, seeing the two firmly against her involvement in the potentially dangerous visit to Rosewood.

"I could wait for you here," she suggested, a note of desperation entering her tone.

"Waiting at a desolate crossroads by yourself is

just asking for trouble," Reza said distractedly. Most of her focus was on the Rosewood tree line that flirted with the rolling fog clouds.

"I can handle myself," Kaia insisted.

Nomad sighed and looked to Reza, who was now completely involved in scoping out their destination as the fogbank let up, giving them their first clear view of the distant church structure.

"You sure you want to do this, Kaia?" he asked. "We can't force you to return home, but I can tell you this; we're sneaking into that place, which they're not going to appreciate, even if they aren't the shady group we think they are. If you get caught in there, we've got no help coming to save us. If you stay the night here, strange cults might be the least of your worries. Travelers seeing a lone, young girl that doesn't know how to protect herself...well, it's like Reza said, that's just asking for trouble."

"There's not enough time to make it back to Glensing before nightfall. I'm camping roadside alone regardless this night. Might as well be at the crossroads, waiting for you two to return."

Nomad let the point sit with him a moment as he looked toward Rosewood.

"This is why I didn't want her to come," Reza grumbled. "She's your responsibility, not mine. You're the one that wanted her to come along. Make your choice if she comes or goes soon. We need to get off the road before we start to look suspicious, and we need to make a plan for our approach."

Nomad nodded. He looked to Kaia, who was giving him her full attention. "We don't know what threats await us in that convent, but...honestly, I'd rather have you with us than out here alone on the open road."

He paused, thinking over his options one last time. "If you promise to stay close to me and do as you're told, you can come."

Her smile was infectious. Nomad smirked back, glad that Reza was too absorbed with picking out a route to witness the moment. He knew the mission would demand their utmost focus and sobriety, but the girl's giddy nature sparked a distant memory of similar occasions between master and pupil in his youth.

The memory of the feeling alone gave him heart. He clapped the girl's back as he settled the matter, then looked to Reza to guide them into Rosewood.

CHAPTER 6 - A HOUSE OF SIN

The fog lingered deep into the night, making visibility far worse than any of them had been expecting. Reza had chosen a surveillance position close to one of the half-built walls along the perimeter of the convent, where they spent the start of the night hunkered down, listening and waiting for activity to cease.

They had gathered two things at the far end of the property in the handful of hours of their stakeout: there were dogs on the premises, and none of the inhabitants spoke the entire time as they had gone about their evening routine.

Thankfully, they had been warned of the dogs' presence by a lengthy and loud quarrel between two of the hounds. As there was no wind, they hoped they were far enough away that neither sound nor smell would alert the hounds of their campout.

They had seen white-robed figures passing between buildings from time to time when the fog had briefly lifted, but they had not heard a word exchanged at any point.

Throughout the years, Reza and Nomad had practiced sign language together, which had come in handy more than a few times during their travels. They signed to each other now, leaving Kaia to only guess what messages were flashing between them.

"Think they've taken a vow of silence?" Nomad asked with his hands.

"Possibly," Reza gestured, thinking how to word her next complex question. She started, slowly at first, picking up speed as she worked through the string of thoughts. "How do we handle the dogs? We should move in now. It is late enough, but the dogs need to be put down first."

"We need to know how many," Nomad signed, and rubbed his chin as he looked across the convent's grounds.

After a moment, he came to a decision. "I'll go handle dogs; you take Kaia and infiltrate the chapel. I'll meet up with you inside."

Reza frowned, not pleased with Nomad dumping Kaia on her already. At the root of it though, she knew the pairing to be the most sensible option. Dogs were tricky to deal with, and if Kaia tagged along with Nomad, they would be alerted before Nomad could take care of the animals. Sneaking around humans was a much easier task. Nomad was stealthier than she.

"Fine," she gestured.

Nomad nodded. "Give me fifteen minutes, then head to the main building."

Nomad stalked off through the brush, disappearing from sight as he crossed over the broken section of wall. Kaia looked at Reza with a questioning look, undecided on if she should follow him or stay with her.

Reza leaned in close to Kaia and whispered into her ear. "He's going to handle the dogs. You're with me. We'll sneak into the inner cloister in a bit. Wait for my mark and stay close once we're on the move."

Kaia nodded, relieved at the update.

Reza could tell the young woman was nervous, as she should be. Though Reza had not liked the idea of the girl coming with them, she forced herself to reset her attitude. Now that Kaia was there, it would only harm the operation if Reza harbored any resentment. Kaia, for the night at least, was part of her unit. Reza could express her grievances with Nomad the following day, but she needed a clear head here and now.

The minutes ticked by, and Reza listened for sounds of alarm as the ten-minute mark elapsed. She knew Nomad would be upon the dogs at that point. At any moment, his cover could be blown, and the convent would be lit up in a swirl of activity.

Thirteen, then fourteen minutes ticked by. She placed a hand on Kaia's forearm to warn her to be ready to move.

A few moments later, Reza was up and moving toward the open archway, Kaia following as quietly and close behind as she could manage. Leaning up against the stone wall, Reza peeked across the sanctuary's grounds, planning a route for them and watching for robed figures. Seeing a route that would offer them partial cover, she nodded to Kaia and crept in through the archway, slinking up a grassy rise and into a line of hedges along the outer cloister's covered walkway.

She was just settling down in a wedge of bushes, with Kaia finding a spot next to her, when they heard a yelp from a dog on the far side of the convent. Reza held her breath and listened intently for any following cries.

A low growl, barely audible, came next, then a short scuffle—then silence.

She waited, looking off in the direction of the dogs. The noises from the scuffle had not been terribly noticeable, but if someone had been listening, an investigation would soon follow.

They had agreed upon their approach to Rosewood earlier that evening. If possible, they would avoid using deadly force. Nomad was a fast and effective grappler, and Reza knew he could subdue a dog handler quickly and quietly if it came to that. However, knocking hostiles unconscious over outright killing them always came with huge liabilities. It would put them on a timer. Before long, their opponents would wake and raise an alarm if not bound and gagged properly, which time did not afford

PAULYODER

for their planned rendezvous.

She tapped Kaia, pulling the girl's attention from listening for signs of dogs, and the two entered under the cloister's open walkway. They approached the entrance to the main chapel.

Reza quietly opened the door and looked in. The chapel's main hall was lined with pews, with a pulpit at the end of the room; candles were lit all along the raised stage. She froze just as she was about to enter. A robed figure rose from the front pew with a lit candle. The figure had their back turned to the door as they knelt at the foot of the stage to light a few thick candles along the pulpit's base.

Reza held a warning hand up to Kaia, ordering her to stay by the door as Reza snuck into the room past rows of empty pews. If the parishioner's cowl had not been up, Reza had no doubt they would have heard her footsteps as she approached, but luck seemed to be on her side as she crept up behind the figure undetected.

She slipped an arm around the figure's neck, binding her arm tight and squeezing as she tucked her head in close to the back of the head of the hooded one.

The victim struggled weakly, but with a flex of her biceps, Reza quickly wrung the fight out of her opponent, and put them to sleep within moments.

Reza eased the figure to the floor. Then she was on them, flipping them over and slapping a hand over their mouth in the next moment, ready for a struggle if the chokehold hadn't completely put them to sleep.

The cloaked figure was limp and didn't struggle against Reza's rough handling. Her heart was pounding loudly in her ears now, but she could still hear Kaia's footsteps approaching. Kaia leaned over the two as Reza studied the face of the woman she had just put under.

The nun's face was ashen and sunken. It was clear she was malnourished. The nun was so gaunt, in fact, that Reza wondered if the strong-arm approach hadn't outright killed her.

"My god," Kaia whispered as Reza slid her hand away from the nun's mouth to reveal stitches that permanently held the nun's lips shut.

"Vow of silence indeed," she muttered, searching for a pulse. Finding her heartbeat, she got to work on disrobing her.

Tossing the white robe to Kaia, Reza ordered in a hushed voice, "Put it on."

Reza flipped the woman over, pulled a thin cord from her belt, and began binding the mute nun's hands and feet behind her.

A crude necklace dangled about the nun's neck as Reza worked. With a sharp tug, she snatched the cord free and inspected the single pearl on the leather strand before pocketing the item.

"Guess we won't need a gag," she said after the

job was done, looking to get a quick read on Kaia.

She had put the robe on as commanded, but the girl was clearly shaken. Reza didn't doubt that the abruptness of the attack had shocked the rookie—she just hoped she'd be able to snap out of it by the time Reza finished placing the body under one of the pews.

Reza finished stashing the nun's limp body out of sight and snuck to the torch-lit hallway at the back of the chapel that looked to lead further into the building. She looked back, seeing Kaia more composed than she had been moments before. She was grateful for that. She didn't need unnecessary complications at this point.

She looked to the chapel's entrance, thinking to wait for Nomad a moment longer, but knew now that they had made their first move, they would be wise to stay mobile. She had no doubt Nomad would catch up to them.

Reza was struggling with the decision of whether to stay or go when Kaia turned and rushed to the chapel's pulpit. Closing the open book on the stand, she hurried back to Reza's side with book in hand.

An anguished cry sounded down the hallway, catching both women's attention, freezing them in place. A door slammed just around the bend. Reza grabbed Kaia and pulled her close. They hugged the wall as they listened to the mournful cries of a woman being dragged away from them down the hallway.

Reza motioned for Kaia to follow her, and the two started down the candle-lit hallway in pursuit.

They came to the door that had been slammed. Reza halted, listening to the retreating footsteps of the person dragging the crying woman further down the hall. Painful yelps paired with thumps against the stone floor suggested they now pulled her downstairs.

Reza tested the handle of the door. Finding it unlocked, she quietly opened it and snuck a peek inside the room.

The sight made her heart drop. It was a holding room filled with women of all ages and races. All were naked, bound to posts or wall anchors, and had cinched blindfolds across their eyes. It was clear that they had been abused, and many showed signs of injury and neglect. Some seemed aware of the door being cracked open, and they trembled violently, looking blindly away from the door as if Reza would, at any moment, rush in to assault them.

"God damn it," Reza cursed under her breath, shutting the door to focus on the sounds of the dying struggle much further down the hall now. She needed to stay focused on the task at hand. The stakes of their surveillance mission had just escalated.

"Were those…women?" Kaia whispered.

Reza clapped a hand over Kaia's mouth as she leaned in to whisper. "We need to know where they're taking that screaming woman. We free that lot in there now and our cover is blown. We'll come back for the rest after we know what the hell they're doing with them."

Holding her hand over Kaia's mouth a moment longer, she looked down the hallway both ways to confirm no one had spotted them. She glared at Kaia a final time to ensure that she didn't contest her decision, then Reza started off down the hallway.

The light faded around the next bend, and the two stopped as they came to a flight of steps that led down into a dark basement tunnel network, paths branching off in multiple directions. The screams were muffled and distant, leaving Reza to guess which tunnel they were emanating from.

They both cautiously descended the flight of stairs, hugging the edge of the wall that turned into the only tunnel that was lit. She turned to Kaia and helped to draw the cowl over her head, dipping the brim of the fabric low to hide most of her visage in shadows.

Leaning in, she whispered into the hood, "If we get separated or spotted, you keep calm and pretend to be a nun. Head back to the surface and get the hell back to Alumin."

A door further down the tunnel opened. Reza turned to try and pinpoint what sounds susurrated from deep within it. Chanting, low and rhythmic, came from further down the tunnel—and screams. They could hear other voices now joining in the pandemonium of agony and fear.

An early memory of occult practices and rites flashed through her head. The horrors of Brigganden and the arisen invasion jolted through her during the brief moment the door had been open. The door slammed shut, and the hall was silent once more, leaving Reza in a cold sweat.

Reza jumped as Kaia placed a worried hand on her arm.

"Change of plans," Reza whispered, her breath quickening with rage and fear from past traumas battling fiercely within her. She was too battle-hardened to allow her fear to win out. By the time she continued her order to Kaia, she had already determined her next line of action.

"You head back up to that room," she started, retrieving a knife from her belt. "Free those girls, and *run immediately* afterward. You understand? You don't stop till you reach Glensing and tell someone what's happening here. After that, you return to West Perch, and you tell the sisterhood."

Kaia hesitated briefly but shored up and nodded. Taking the book and knife in either hand, Kaia turned and rushed back up the stairs, leaving Reza alone in the dark of the expansive basement.

Reza watched her go, then turned back to her task. She made her way down the domed tunnel, which ended in a small alcove. A few candles lit the shrines on either side of two double doors. Moans and occasional cries sounded from within.

She was about to turn the door handle when she took a second glance at the clutter upon the base of the shrine. Along the shelf lay more corded pearl necklaces, and on the floor lay a few disheveled white robes, similar to the one they had taken from the nun in the chapel.

Her mind raced to make sense of the scene they had glimpsed so far. The convent seemed to be operating as a human meat market. Whether they were ordaining more mouthless nuns within the ceremony room beyond the doors or simply slaughtering scores of helpless women, she couldn't say. Regardless, she hoped to soon find out. Her hands ached to strangle someone.

Snatching the stash of necklaces and shoving them in her side pouch, she grabbed a white robe from the pile and threw it over her trail clothes, tugging the hood low. She carefully unsheathed her longsword and hid it in the folds of her robe. Grabbing the door handle, she took a deep breath, opened the door, and crossed the threshold as fresh screams filled the hall.

CHAPTER 7 - NIGHT OF HELL

The room was dim and smoky; a stale incense haze hung in the air like gossamer. Reza slowly closed the door behind her and waited for her eyes to adjust to the gloom.

A shrill scream startled her, causing her to turn as a frantic, naked woman rushed at her. The woman lunged at Reza but tripped a stride away and slammed into the cold, stone floor.

Reza thought the woman was oddly quiet, but then she noticed a gurgling sound. The woman was starting to convulse, struggling to control her body.

Reza backed against the door as the woman began vomiting profusely on the filth-smeared floor. Then, with her eyes adjusting to the light of the candle-lit room, Reza saw that it was not vomit the woman spewed up but fleshy entrails throbbing into a coiled mass at Reza's feet.

She stood still, watching as the woman's insides expelled themselves through her mouth until her skin itself violently ripped through the fiendish maw that wrapped around and over her face. All that was left at the end of the nightmarish episode was a steaming pile of pulsing gore on the floor of the dark ceremonial room.

Reza gasped a ragged breath of the moldy air in, doing all she could to ward off flashbacks of the countless mangled bodies she had seen in her many years embroiled in war. Try as she might to control her presence of mind, the scene had struck a painfully intense chord.

A man approached, also nude but covered in blood. His face was one massive, angry scar, his eyes plucked out. He turned to Reza and seemed to look directly at her for a moment, his empty sockets unsettling her. The moment passed, and he reverently knelt and scooped up the mound of raw flesh.

Reza simply watched, still too shocked by the scene she had walked in on to have sense enough to take in the rest of the room and come up with a plan.

She was not sure if she could trust her eyes at that point, but as the man turned, Reza thought she saw his scorched hand flicker, disappear, and then return.

"What are you doing down here?" a white-robed man asked as he approached her, snapping her from her daze.

Stooping her head to hide her mouth, she bowed to the clergyman and offered the stack of robes.

His voice was thin, nasally. "We've already got enough robes; only a few are taking their vows this day. What about the Breath of Life? Did you bring more of those?"

Reza hesitated, head still submissively bowed to hide her mouth.

"The prayer beads, did you bring them?" he asked impatiently.

She fumbled through her robes and handed over the tangle of pearl necklaces.

"I'll get these to the reverend father. He'll be handling the novitiates soon. First, the flesh offerings."

The man turned to watch the naked, bloodied man who approached a dark statue at the center of the room. Reza followed his gaze, studying the ritual circle intently. Her eyes fixated upon the bundle of flesh that the naked man carried, which was all that was left of the woman who had stumbled at her feet moments ago. The mass still pulsed and writhed. Reza grimly wondered if the woman somehow still lived after the grotesque transformation.

The father stood before the glistening obsidian figure, handing the twitching flesh cluster over to the open arms of the statue. The room reverently quieted, even the moans and cries dying down as all now stood transfixed upon the scene. Somehow, all could sense the importance of the moment.

Reza couldn't tear her eyes away from the statue and the knot of flesh. The more she focused, the more her vision played tricks on her. Fleeting images of the ambiguously gendered dark figure inverted, and in different places it glistened with blackness and pearlescent colors that flickered all about the dark totem. The bundle of flesh, now in the statue's embrace, began to morph. The woman's face stretched out of the intestinal wall, locked in a soundless scream of agony.

The moment itself became distorted, like a kaleidoscope of space and time. Reza's mind warped in on itself, her mind popping like a soapy bubble that had grown too large to sustain its surface area. Identity drained from her as other strange and foreign identities flooded into her. She became aware of many things in that moment—the subconscious of all in the room passing through her and her through them.

She was aware of screams. She wasn't sure if the screams were those of the other naked women in the room, the mass of faces stretching out of the thin membrane of flesh upon the altar of obsidian hands, or her own screams of horror.

The moment of madness passed as the flesh blinked away in a dark flash of iridescence, leaving in its place a small pearl in the palm of the figure. The statue itself seemed to breathe a slow breath of relief before returning to its inanimate self.

Her head was yanked back. The man next to her ripped her hood down. They had marked her, she knew, just as she now understood the secrets of

Rosewood and the horrors of what the dark statue represented. For all her grit, she trembled, frozen in the clutches of the Torchbearer as the man strung an arm around her neck, holding her in place. The reverend father turned to consider the tainted heathen in the holiest of their ceremonies.

The Torchbearer tightened his lock on her neck as the reverend father moved toward her. Her eyes bulged from the strain, but the pain of the choke snapped her from her shock, and she elbowed the man in the ribs hard enough to take the wind from him. His grip loosened, allowing Reza to drop her stance and hurl him over her hip and onto the dusty floor.

The room exploded into pandemonium. Torchbearers and the uninitiated alike either rushed to detain Reza or tried to escape. The reverend father's eyeless gaze was locked on Reza through all the chaos.

Reza was only distantly aware of the light that spilled into the room as the doors flew open. Shouts issued from Torchbearers close to her, rushing after the naked women who were fleeing toward the lone figure at the door's threshold.

Reza tore her gaze from the bloody father to look back to the exit. She saw a very disheveled Nomad backing into the room, his full attention on something down the tunnel from which he came.

A feeble man's hand gripped Reza's arm. She went for her sword. Steel glinted in the candlelight as she slashed through the elderly Torchbearer's wrist, severing it cleanly, leaving the man screaming as she spurred into motion toward Nomad.

Nomad tumbled out of the way just before a chair flew in through the doorway, blasting apart as it hit the floor several meters behind him. The crowd of sacrificial women milled in panic, trapped between the horrors of the altar and the hulk lumbering in from the tunnel. It only just fit the space because of its hunched and malformed shoulder.

The giant was disfigured, streaked with iridescent light all along its back and arms. Scars riddled its face and limbs, and in the light, Reza couldn't tell if the abomination was a natural defect or a twisted creation of the cult. Whichever it was, Reza now understood why Nomad had been late to their rendezvous.

The giant man snatched up a woman by the waist and hurled her at Nomad. Nomad rolled out of the way again, the helpless woman skipping off the stone with a sickening crack of bones. The dodge had left Nomad off balance, and the hulk rushed him and swung an arm thick as a tree trunk. It clipped Nomad across the shoulder, sending him tumbling toward Reza.

She held out her free hand to catch him, and the two crashed to the ground with the brute rushing toward them.

A bloodied hand rested upon Reza as she came to her senses. The soft voice of the father, speaking in tongues that were oddly familiar, spewed from his mouth like invisible worms, writhing into her brain. Her body started to undulate and pulse with every syllable of the otherworldly prayer.

Nomad was up, moving fast to snatch Reza from the man's grasp. He tugged her out of the way just as the hulk crashed through. The barreling hunchback bowled into the bloodied father, knocking him across the room and into the obsidian statue so forcefully that it rocked back, then tipped over and shattered into a million splinters of glistening crystal.

Reza's mind, which moments earlier had felt like mush, suddenly returned to her, and she picked up her pace as Nomad dragged her toward the open doorway. The hulk looked stupidly at the father, wondering if it should come to the father's aid or give chase to the small man it had been pursuing for the last few minutes. They didn't wait around for it to decide. Nomad slammed both doors shut on the room of horrors.

"We need to leave," Nomad panted. "Where's Kaia?"

Reza slashed into the back of a Torchbearer who was struggling with one of the girls, kicking him off her as she yelled back to Nomad, "She's upstairs!"

Nomad helped the naked girl up but could see that she struggled to stand, a broken or twisted ankle bending her over in pain.

He sheathed his sword and hefted her over his

shoulders. She cried out but allowed the stranger to carry her, apparently aware that they were not with the cultists.

The doors down the tunnel crashed open. Nomad pressed Reza up the stairs, not even bothering to look back at the giant in pursuit.

"Here," Nomad shouted at the top of the stairs as he handed the girl over to Reza. "Find Kaia and get as many as you can out of here. I'll give you some time."

Reza didn't have time to sheath her sword. She fumbled to awkwardly hold the bundle of a girl in her arms, wanting to argue the point with Nomad even as she saw the silhouette of the devilishly fast hunchback barreling down the tunnel toward them.

She turned and ran, blasting past the empty holding room and into the chapel now rife with activity.

"Kaia!" Reza called, seeing a Torchbearer struggling with the young saren, a group of frightened naked women behind her.

Reza started toward them to help the girl fend off the man, but as she approached them, she saw the Torchbearer jerk and go rigid. Kaia pushed him off her. The knife Reza had given her was lodged to the hilt just under the man's ribs.

It would be a slow death, Reza thought as she stepped over the man's pain-wracked face.

"We need to leave," Reza told the women. No one argued with her. Kaia sprung to open the chapel door leading into the cloister.

Screams sounded in the cold of the night; it was apparent they were not the only ones fleeing the grounds. The Torchbearers were out in force, working to contain the pandemonium and stop more sacrifices from escaping.

Reza handed the girl over to Kaia and ordered her to go on ahead to the road. Turning her attention to the three Torchbearers who had closed in on their group, Reza paced their line a moment, waiting for them to make their move.

Only one held a weapon, but that did not seem to worry the other two in the least. The one with the crude sword came in at Reza. His inexperienced, wide swing left him open for Reza to redirect and strike him in the chest, puncturing his lung.

Even in his frenzy, the strike clearly fazed the man. With the fatal wound of their comrade on display, the other two rushed her, slamming her into the brush to the side of the path. She pitched one over into the bushes, but the other tore at her face with his hands, attempting to bite her.

Reza kneed the savage man in the groin and smashed her elbow into the side of his head, dazing him for a moment. She was about to strike him again when a sword point burst through his chest, the other man hoping to get at her through his own comrade.

The point didn't have enough length, and she flung the dead man off her, along with the buried sword, and slashed up at the disarmed Torchbearer.

He crumpled to the ground, his throat opened by the tip of Reza's longsword. She was up and running the next moment, wiping tears from her eyes, a scratch across her eye leaving a terrible sting.

She heard a chant start up behind her, and she was just turning to regard the noise when the sensation of her face starting to tear in half stopped her in her tracks. She tried to clutch at her burning face. The chanting grew louder as the Torchbearer steadily approached.

She screamed in pain—in fear—and slashed out with her sword toward the sound, which had begun to lose its tether to one particular location, seeming to be all around her now.

As the pain reached its crescendo, Reza felt as though the scratch left by the cultist was opening deeper and deeper, rending her skull. She flailed with her sword, and the chanting suddenly turned to a gurgle. The pain receded. Reza realized she had buried her longsword deep in the head of the mutated singer.

She yanked the blade free of the warped figure and forced herself to turn and run, breath coming back to her in sharp gasps as her body started to obey her commands bit by bit.

She stumbled out onto the muddy trail that led back to the highway. She said a thankful prayer to Sareth as she spotted Kaia's group further up ahead. Reza was gasping for air at that point, almost mindlessly huffing along as she tried to clear her head of the haze that had overcome her.

She was exhausted and confused, but as she looked to the crossroads once more, she saw tall figures in the dark of the night approaching the group of naked women. She rushed ahead, sword out with the single intent to defend the group with what strength she had left in her.

She crashed through a row of brush toward the looming figures that stood over Kaia's group and was distantly aware of orders being shouted.

"There," a horseman said, another rider taking aim and thudding an arrow into Reza's shoulder. The impact caused her to drop her sword. She fell, tumbling in a daze out onto the road like a downed animal.

"Reza!" she heard Kaia cry.

"Another damned White Cloak. Shut that other one up," she heard a man say as one of the figures dismounted, coming to her.

As he bent to grab her, she backhanded him squarely across the face. The next moment, an impact shook her world. A flash of stars burst through her vision—then blackness.

CHAPTER 8 - UNDER AN APPLE TREE

A sharp pain in her head and arm caused her to wince as she came to. She was sitting in a saddle, the steady rhythm of a horse trot slowly nudging her awake. She was being held up by an arm loosely draped over her midsection.

She must have moaned or tensed up, for the rider holding her from behind started to speak in a calm, direct voice. "We all saw what you did to the general last night. Don't give us any more reason to distrust you."

She stilled at the comment even though she wanted to look at her shoulder, which felt like it was on fire. Fully conscious now, she considered her options. The silence prompted the man holding her to continue. "You're in no immediate danger here. We'll even patch up that shoulder once we stop, but if you act up, you will be forced into shackles."

Reza opened her eyes, seeing that the sun was well into the noon-day sky. She was on horseback, riding in the midst of a company, twenty or thirty strong. She would have little to no chance of making an escape, even if her situation was dire, which it didn't yet appear to be.

By the looks of the organized company and the tall and slender haltia making up the bulk of the troop, Reza guessed she rode now with some Silver Streams cavalry unit. Whether they were a private or military force, she had no idea.

The horse picked up the pace, and they moved close to another rider who wore a double stack tiara, simple in design yet elegant.

"Colonel," Reza's rider said, grabbing the haltia's attention. "The one who struck the general is awake."

Reza's stomach churned at the line, faintly recalling, with a great deal of effort, the insanity of the previous night; the sting of an arrow in her shoulder, slugging the figure over her, a blinding impact before she had blacked out. Much of the night's events were still hazy.

The haltia colonel looked Reza over. "If you had backhanded *me* like that, I'd have left that arrow buried in place all the way to Lancasteal."

She and her rider were silent.

"We'll stop to rest and water the horses soon," the colonel continued. "The general wishes to have a word with you and the other White Cloak."

"I'm no White Cloak, neither is Kaia," Reza corrected.

He glanced her way. "Your robes say otherwise. I know White Cloak attire when I see it. Anyway, it's not my job to judge the validity of your claims. The general wishes to talk with you and the other one himself. I've a feeling he's not too happy about that welt you left on him."

The three rode in silence for a time before the colonel spoke again. "Jake, make sure she behaves the next few miles till we stop for a rest. Take her to General Seldrin then. Go and find the other one while you're at it—bring them both. You keep an eye on them when they're with him, you hear? If she ends up bruising another haltia this day...I'll handle her personally."

"Yes sir," Reza's rider answered and trotted back into his spot in the formation.

The ride was quiet the next few miles, which Reza appreciated, since she could spend that time to collect her thoughts. Much of the previous day was still a blur, and her head still throbbed from the trauma she had put her body and mind through the previous night.

The climax of the ceremony had been a deluge of confusing revelations of the cult's identity. She had seen things...experienced multiple different lives. She couldn't sort through any of it just then, she knew. She wasn't even sure that she'd ever be able to unpack what had happened in that dark room, but she felt that there was a key there to unlock some of the mystery behind the cult and their motives. She needed to try to dig into the experience and discuss things with Nomad.

Later, she thought as the group headed toward a rough-looking orchard, perhaps tended to in years past but gone to seed recently.

What was more pressing on her mind at that point was Nomad's location and condition. When she had left him, he was heading off to distract the rampaging hunchback all on his own. That Nomad was an exceptional fighter and survivor was undisputed, but Reza had rarely seen such an unbridled beast. The thing's speed was the concerning factor. To be so powerful *and* fast made her worry for her missing companion. She needed to find a way to convince this *General Seldrin* to let her and Kaia go so that she could return to search for Nomad.

Her rider broke from formation once more and found the soldier that was riding with Kaia. Jake called for his fellow soldier to follow. The two horses trotted out of the pack toward the sparse tree line nearby.

Passing under some shady apple trees and past an abandoned orchard shed, they came upon the colonel, who was conversing with another haltia sitting on an old stool at the base of the largest apple tree in the whole orchard.

The colonel's mood hadn't changed since last Reza had seen him, a slight scowl ever on his brow. Her rider came to a stop a respectable distance away, and Kaia's rider pulled up next to them.

"Kaia, you alright?" Reza asked.

"I'm fine, Reza—but your arm! I could perform a healing if they allow it—"

Reza shook her head. "A healing would only sap strength from you. I can handle myself on the road as long as this doesn't get infected. Save your strength."

"Hey," Jake interrupted softly. "Looks like the general is calling you over."

Dismounting, Jake moved to help Reza down from the horse since she wasn't able to hold any weight with her arm. The soldiers walked the two over to the large apple tree.

"Behave yourself, or he'll be turning you over to me," the colonel warned Reza as he took his leave, heading back to tend to the rest of the company.

Reza ignored the comment, focusing instead on the haltia at the base of the apple tree. His features had all the hallmarks of his kind: high cheekbones, an intense brow, and curved ears. His eyes were striking, even for a haltia, who were well known to have colorful irises. They were a light emerald green, speckled with gold flecks that caught the occasional glimmer of light that made its way through the apple tree canopy. A natural dusting of golden freckles graced his brow, and his hair, though brown for the most part, had metallic streaks like veins of gold.

At first glance, the man seemed relaxed, resting from what must have been a long journey, considering that they would have been up all through the night and the morning as well. There was something deeper than exhaustion about his expression. Having been around soldiers and in the military herself for a good decade now, she could spot a veteran. One that had been through the system long enough to have learned to cope with the constant drain and strain of a high-stress environment...and the polish of youthful hope of changing the world thoroughly tarnished. She wondered if Kaia saw the same careworn attitude in herself.

"Have a seat," the man offered, indicating the worn bench across from him.

Reza and Kaia accepted the invitation. The soldiers hovered close behind.

"Jake, Neri, you're dismissed. Go tend to your horses," the general said as he sat up to consider the two women.

They hesitated for a moment, knowing their colonel would lay into them later, but obeyed the superior officer's order and made their way back to their horses. They only retreated to the orchard's perimeter so as to keep the three within view.

The haltia eyed the two saren, studying their attire and searching their eyes. At length, he ordered them to take off their robes.

Kaia obliged, but Reza silently refused.

He gestured for Kaia to hand over her garment, which she did, and he turned it over in his hands, inspecting the knit and make, then looked to Reza.

"Your shoulder hurts?" he asked.

"What do you think? I had an arrow in it last night," she replied.

He smirked. "Perhaps we could start with introductions. I'm Amare Seldrin, general of the Silver Crowns military."

"What is a general doing out in the countryside? For that matter, why were you poking about Rosewood?" Reza asked.

"Where you come from, do generals never venture outside of the capital's walls?" he asked. Seeing that Reza had no answer, he continued. "The Silver Crowns have been in constant hearings and councils in Alumin this last year. Myself and other high-ranking officials have been on the road more than we'd like of late."

Reza thought on the statement for a moment. "And Rosewood? That's the church's land, is it not? Why were you there?"

"We were just setting up camp at the crossroads when a hellish racket alerted my men. My watchmen reported the noise was coming from the nunnery. We came to investigate. It sounded like women were being slaughtered. Our rightful land or not, we weren't going to just camp by the roadside while screams sounded unanswered."

Reza nodded approvingly.

"Now, I've leveled with you. I expect you to do

the same for me. That's the least you could do after giving me this shiner last night," he said, turning his face to give them a clear look at the welt from Reza's backhand. "You were the only two with White Cloak robes on in that group we gathered—the only two *clothed,* for that matter."

"Are the other women alright?" Kaia interrupted. "It was dark when you separated us. I haven't seen them all day. What did you do with them?"

The general raised a hand. "Some were injured —*all* malnourished. They needed medical attention quickly. I sent a lightning squad up ahead. They should already be to Lancasteal by now."

"Why did you not send us with them?" Reza asked, pointing to the rough patch job of bloodied gauze over her shoulder wound.

"You wear White Cloak robes," he answered. "For all I know, you're the cause of those women's condition."

"We're not with them. We had reason to believe Rosewood was involved in some heinous practices. We were infiltrating their operation," Reza refuted. She wished to say more, but for the time being, she knew that the less said to a government official, the better.

He looked over the two women and grunted. "I might believe you. We've looked through your belongings. You'll get your personal effects back once you're cleared, but among your stuff was this emblem from the young miss's pack."

He produced Kaia's West Perch brooch and tossed it back to her.

"I'm guessing you're both saren? What business does West Perch have with Elendium's sect? Were you there under an official capacity?"

"I'm with West Perch," Kaia volunteered. "And yes, we're saren."

Reza held her tongue, but Seldrin could see that she was not happy with Kaia's confession. She didn't like giving up information about themselves so readily, though she didn't see that they had any other choice.

"You said you were infiltrating Rosewood. Were you there on orders?" he circled back.

"No," Reza said, finally giving up. "We heard unsettling things about the operation they're running there. We went there on our own volition. West Perch doesn't know of our involvement."

"Vigilantes?" Seldrin mused. "And it was just you two?"

"No, actually, I wanted to ask you," Reza said, her tone softening. "A foreign man was with us— goes by the name of Nomad. Did any of your men see him last night? He was wearing Southern Sand style clothing."

"Only found you pair and eight hysterical, naked women. Some of my men saw other figures running off across the plains, but we did not pursue," Seldrin answered.

Reza had figured as much, guessing that Nomad would be numbered among them if he had been seen.

"He's a dear friend; we need to return to make sure he made it out of there unharmed. You saw the state of those women. They're doing terrible things there. If they captured him—" She stopped herself, worrying that her emotions would betray her composure.

Seldrin listened intently to Reza's words and paused to consider the request. The hesitation worried Reza.

"I'm not convinced you're associated with the White Cloaks. I believe your story, for the most part. However, in cases like this, I'm obligated to bring all suspicious actors before the magistrates in Lancasteal."

"So, we're your prisoners?" Reza asked.

"You could see yourselves as such. However you term it, you are under my care until I get you before the magistrates. If what you say about Rosewood is true, then this could be a good thing for everyone. Perhaps you could sway Lancasteal officials to finally take action. I, for one, would approve and support the notion. They've been holding a non-interventionist position with the church for far too long, by my account."

"Nomad is missing," she reiterated.

"Then you had better make a convincing case to the judges on why Silver Crowns should intervene with the church's handling of Rosewood," Seldrin concluded.

The haltia allowed Reza to fume over the verdict a moment before ordering her to approach him. She didn't budge.

"Come," he said again, firmer this time, and Reza resentfully obeyed.

"Kneel so I can see your shoulder wound," he said in a softer tone, unstrapping a satchel at his hip. He unfolded it to reveal a stash of medical supplies.

"You're a general *and* a medic?" Reza said wryly.

He looked at her and said with a deadly calm, "Kneel, saren. I'll not ask you again."

She did not hide her frown from him this time but obeyed.

Kaia watched the display wide-eyed.

"No thrashing when I take that robe off, understood? I'll not have another black eye from you."

He was gentle, seeing that the wound was binding her arm in place. He realized that it was likely the reason for such a stubborn display of keeping her robes on when he had asked her to remove them. He doubted that she could manage the robe over her shoulders without aid but was too proud to admit it.

She held back the pain as best she could, but a few grunts gave her away as he finished peeling off the fabric from her wound. He undressed the bandage and exposed the wound to get a look at the state of her injury.

"Looks deep enough, but seems the tip sliced with the grain of the muscle, not through it. That'll mean a quick recovery time if we can stop infection from taking root," he mumbled as he dabbed a clear liquid, patting the stinging astringent along the incision.

His touch was tender but efficient. It was clear that he had practiced hands. Reza eased up a bit, allowing him to treat her without resistance.

"Most generals I know carry weapons, not medical kits," she grumbled, doing her best to endure through the socially uncomfortable position he was putting her in.

"You know many generals?" he asked idly as he wiped the rest of the exposed flesh clean. He looked into her eyes for a moment, considering the thought, then returned to his kit. "I wouldn't doubt it in your case. It's clear you're no ordinary woman."

Pulling out a thread and needle, he looked to make sure she was prepared for him to start with her stitches before pricking her. She grimaced slightly at the first one. He kept the conversation going to keep her mind off the task.

"I was a medic long ago, at the start of my

military career. I kept up with it as I gained rank. Found it to be a nice touchpoint with my troop. No better way to show your soldiers you care than tending to their wounds. It's brought me much trust from those under my command over the years. A good trade-off, I'd say. Fewer headaches for you when your company has your back."

He snipped the thread and took out a mash of white powder. He sprinkled some on a clean patch of gauze and placed it over the wound, then bound it under and over Reza's shoulder, tucking it tight into her armpit, which caused her to squirm slightly at the ticklish intrusion.

Seldrin smiled to himself. He appreciated the fact that of all the pain the saren had endured through the dressing, the thought of revealing that she was ticklish was the most uncomfortable thing she had to endure.

Reza glanced at Kaia to find the youth smiling warmly at the unexpected kindness from the military leader.

Reza carefully eased back into the sleeve of her travel vest. The fresh bandage did wonders to cut down on the discomfort that had been biting at her that whole morning.

In spite of his troops being the ones that had shot her in the first place, she managed a "thank you" to the general for providing her and Kaia with more than what most war leaders would have the decency to offer.

He got up and plucked a few apples from the bountiful tree, offering them both one.

"Better than trail rations," he said, taking a bite of his.

Reza pocketed hers for later and snagged another from the tree to snack on.

"You'll ride tandem with me so I can keep an eye on that shoulder," Seldrin said as he led them back to the orchard's tree line.

The general seemed a reasonable enough man, certainly one with sympathies somewhat uncommon in his rank, but she knew his word was final—regardless of whether she objected to the offer.

Though it seemed that they were not in any immediate danger in the company of the Silver Crowns troop, the fact of the matter was that they were headed in the opposite direction she wished to go. They were leaving Nomad behind to his fate.

They rode in silence the first few miles, the general's arms resting on either side of Reza's waist. Typically, when she had rode tandem, she was the back rider, but haltias were some of the lighter of races in Una, and she understood the need to keep the heavier weight off the horse's loins.

"You never gave me your name," Seldrin pointed out, breaking the silence.

"You never demanded it of me, why would I have freely given it to my captor?" she grumbled.

"You know, some would say that we saved you and those abused women back at that crossroads," he replied.

"I had a handle on the situation. We didn't need your troop to come storming in just then."

"You spilled out of those bushes like a wild beast, panting and about to keel over," he argued. She did not respond, and he cursed under his breath, "A handle on the situation, my ass. Obstinate woman."

She was silent over the insult for a moment.

He sighed. "I'm sorry. I'm sure you're just worried about your *Nomad* friend."

"Yes, I am, and I wish to return to search for him."

This time it was his turn to remain silent.

They rode for many more miles. Seldrin occasionally received reports from his officers as the company strolled along the picturesque grassy countryside, fluffy white clouds passing overhead occasionally to provide them with some shade.

"Reza," she offered as they trotted along up a slope of road.

"Pardon?" he asked, navigating around some rocks in the path.

"My name is Reza."

He shifted in his saddle and asked, more than a little bewildered at the claim, "Not Reza Malay by chance?"

Reza broke out in a cold sweat. She was not pleased at all with the general, so far from her homeland, knowing her just by her first name. She nodded.

"Well, well. At least in military circles, you're something of a war hero. By my understanding, Southern Sands would be well in the throes of a siege if it weren't for you and your company."

It was clear he was impressed with her. She wondered if Sultan Metus, Judge Hagus, Colonel Durmont, or some other important figure of the Southern Sands had spread word about her involvement in the war. She supposed she would have to follow up with her connections once back in her homeland and ask them to refrain from spreading her name around. She had never wished to be famous or revered—though, likely, the damage had already been done. She could not force them to take back her popularity, she supposed. At the least, from what she had heard from Kaia, the reports put her in a good light.

"If that's the case, your story is starting to make a lot more sense to me," he said as they crested the rise.

A breeze with grassy notes mingled with freshwater scents rushed past them, rousing them and their steed as they halted. Reza couldn't help but smile at the beauty of the scene. At the bottom of the valley lay a massive lake that touched along the borders of a spread-out metropolis that seemed to blend right into the distant tree lines to the south.

The sweeping spired green and blue castle tops at the far end of the lovely city of Lancasteal were a sight to behold. High bridges and walkways ran along the tops of the towers and tall structures, giving dimension to the grandiose castle district.

"Ever been to Lancasteal?" Seldrin asked as he snapped the reins to start his horse moving again.

"No," Reza admitted, the sight causing her to momentarily forget about her ongoing feud with the man.

She held onto the horn of the saddle, taking in the vista as they clopped along. She added, quite distracted, "Nor the Silver Crowns kingdom for that matter."

"There's no place like it in the neighboring kingdoms. It is a place close to all haltias' hearts."

"No wonder haltias aren't big travelers. I've only ever known a few. With a homeland like this, why would they ever wish to leave?"

Seldrin considered her thoughts. "Look close enough at paradise, and you will always find flaws. No place is perfect, even Lancasteal for all its splendor. Still, it is my home, and by no means a terrible place to live. Your hearing will take place there," he said, pointing to a huge court building at the center of the castle district. "I'll escalate your case; bring it to the higher circuit. You'll speak before the board of high judges. Hopefully, you can express your concern about the crimes being committed at Rosewood without offending too many officials."

The rest of the company was catching up to them now, and she could hear the occasional cheer from the score of horse riders that peaked the hilltop as they beheld their homeland.

"Keep a head about you. They'll not be as lenient with your fiery tongue as I have been. Mind yourself," he warned.

There was a bit of sarcasm in her voice when she asked, "Is this the usual protocol for handling *suspicious actors* found roadside? To bring them before the high judges?"

"No."

She was about to ask why he was involving himself in what he had deemed to be a standard procedural affair, but she decided not to. It was clear he had his reasons. It had sounded to her as though he was not happy with his own government's treatment of the contested property that the church operated at the edge of their borders. Perhaps he wished its investigation to be seriously dealt with.

Instead, she asked, "What will become of me after my hearing?"

"Depends on how your hearing goes, but I'd guess, knowing who you are and that haltias respect the sarens, you'll be released and allowed to return to search for your Nomad friend."

She thought upon his words for a time as they trotted along the peaceful country road leading to the farmlands outside of the city proper. The country air had helped clear her mind. She had been focused on Nomad throughout most of the day, but the door to that course was closed for the time being, at least until she dealt with the court system in Lancasteal. As that was her immediate task, she needed to focus on what lay ahead of her.

Rosewood, and the things connected to the cult that operated there, was almost certainly part of the bigger picture of the threat Lanereth had warned her of in the four kingdoms. The White Cloaks were connected with the church of Elendium in some direct way—she knew that now. Many locals seem to understand this, yet the officials from any kingdom remained resistant to do anything about it. Why that was the case was an issue to delve into deeper all on its own.

She was being handed an audience with some of the most powerful representatives of the Silver Crowns kingdom. She needed to appreciate the opportunity for what it was and direct her attention to obtaining information while she had the chance, and to present her case clearly before a body of influential members that could become allies to her cause.

"Will Kaia be brought with me?" Reza asked hopefully.

"I'd assume so, yes. I'll have to give my initial report and see what they're willing to permit."

"Please allow us to share quarters and attend the hearing together. We're a unit."

"I'll do what I can," Seldrin answered.

She knew she wasn't the best with negotiations; she was aware of her weakness when dealing with bureaucrats. Kaia, on the other hand, potentially was of use in that department. She hoped the young saren was good at her job. There were no do-overs with audiences—as West Perch had painfully reminded her.

CHAPTER 9 - LANCASTEAL

The stunning haltia city design had not been lost on Reza. It was the most welcoming, gorgeous city she had ever seen—on the surface at least. She was no bumpkin. She knew that every city, no matter how clean and healthy it seemed, had its fair share of problems, even if not easily discernible to a passerby.

The troop had escorted her and Kaia all the way to the sweeping skyline castles, joined high up by an elegant network of bridges. The forest canopy had been incorporated into the architecture to bring out a more natural beauty to the grandiose structures, which likely would look daunting without the fluff of green the tall trees dispersed through the grounds provided.

She had kept silent and to herself through most of the trip. Kaia had looked as though she wished to talk with her, either for comfort or to get on the same page with their story and defense. The colonel had made sure they were separated for that exact reason —so they could not corroborate before they gave their testimonies.

They halted at a large platform at the base of the central castle tower and waited for Seldrin to give orders to his troop. He sent most off, only keeping the colonel, Jake, and Neri in his company.

They boarded the platform. A lift attendant signaled up to the pulley operators, and the platform steadily began to climb flight after flight until they were at the top. They disembarked onto a large bridge walkway leading them to the main governance keep. At that time of evening, the walkway was busy with the end of the workday rush.

Reza looked down off the platform to get a bird's eye view of the commerce and upscale marketing districts below. The commerce grounds were even more bustling, and even after a tug from the colonel who was escorting her, she still stole some peeks at the fairgrounds that were rife with merriment and music that she could hear, even from high up as they were.

They entered the grand city hall's lobby. The attendants and workers met the general with warm welcomes as he led Reza, Kaia, and the remaining members of his troop up a flight of stairs and down a hall of chambers.

"Jake, Neri, you'll be on constant watch for these two till I can schedule them in the docket for tonight or tomorrow's court sessions," Seldrin announced as they came to two empty chambers halfway down the hall. "We'll house them in a guest suite, one to a room."

"We have cells for this sort of thing," the colonel

grumbled.

"It wouldn't behoove us to jail dignitaries from allied states, would it, Colonel Rupert?" Seldrin said. "Unless you are the one to explain to both West Perch and the Plainstate why we didn't treat two of their esteemed representatives with respect during their stay with us."

"That's who *they* say they are," the colonel murmured.

"I doubt they're making up such specific claims, but if they are, it'll come out at the hearing soon enough."

Reza allowed the two to finish bickering before commenting, "I'd like my things if that's possible."

"Out of the question," the colonel glowered, and even Seldrin seemed tired at the request.

"Please, just our packs, not our weapons. I'd like to have access to my books at least," she explained.

Seldrin considered the request before turning his attention to the two soldiers still with them. "Jake and Neri, take inventory of their packs first. Have the weapons, tools, and suspicious items sent to my quarters for safe keeping."

It was clear she held no favor with the colonel, but acquiring most of their gear meant they could at least remain productive if they were forced to wait indefinitely for a court meeting. Kaia had the book from the pulpit to pore over, and Reza needed to record key events from the last few days and attempt to make sense of it all on paper. It might also give her time to memorize some of the maps in the kingdom boundaries book Kaia had given to her.

"Yes sir." Both soldiers saluted and carried the packs into the separate rooms.

Seldrin nodded, then turned back to Colonel Rupert. "Colonel, let's leave them to it. We've got some scheduling to do and reports to prepare."

The soldiers led Reza and Kaia into their respective rooms and proceeded to sort through their packs. Reza did appreciate that Jake was being careful with her belongings. She had nothing sensitive, either in content or design, that she worried over. She knew her sword and dagger would be taken, which they were. Everything else passed his check, though, and before long, Neri had finished her check of Kaia's gear, keeping back just the camp knife Reza had given her the night before.

"I'll get these to general's quarters double time if you keep an eye on them both for a bit," Jake offered, which Neri agreed to.

Reza and Kaia were forced to keep their doors open while Neri watched them both, but that didn't stop Reza from organizing her pack and taking out a small leatherbound trail journal. Luckily for her, there was a writing desk in her room, and she popped open the ink well, took out a quill, and slowed her mind to consider where to begin.

She dipped her quill in the ink pot and penned a fresh line at the start of the page.

Though I've endured and bore witness to many trials of the flesh and not a few of the horrors of war and hell, last night nearly broke my mind and identity. Whatever force it was that warped my grasp on reality greatly worries me. For the first time in a long time, I am afraid.

You have my account of heeding Lanereth's call and my time in Alumin and West Perch in the previous pages of this journal, so I'll not backtrack. I'll start with our investigation of Rosewood.

Our hunch proved to be correct. The church of Elendium is known to own that parcel of land, and the cult known as the White Cloaks have been operating the facility there for some time now. The two are connected: the church and this upstart cult. Many locals seem to understand vague details, but there is a sort of hush on the topic. There are rumors, there are warnings, but no clear answers that we've been given thus far.

I infiltrated their convent with Nomad and Kaia. They were keeping women locked in dungeons, naked and abused. They were taking them down into their basement chapel to perform some sort of anointing ceremony. I interceded and beheld a forbidden vision—if vision is the correct term for it.

My mind seemed to spill out of me, and at the same time, it was filled with the consciousnesses of the sacrificial women, the Torchbearers, and the reverend father in the room. We merged for a split moment in time. It was at once a flash and an eternity.

Their cause is terrible and dangerous, and worse, I fear it is widespread throughout the kingdoms. I suspect these White Cloaks have been a joint sect of Elendium for some time now, working under the shroud of secrecy, biding their time as the church acts as a front for them.

I'm not sure of any of this; the thoughts I received were horribly muddled—hence why I felt it imperative to record as much as I could here and now. It was like a vivid dream. Once I awoke, the memories that were so real just moments ago seemed to fade quickly like mist in the morning sun. Now, I'm mostly left with feelings.

A single, firm detail about the whole experience remains: I should fear the one they called Umbraz— the dark statue in the cursed underground chapel room. Perhaps it could be simply a fraction of it or an icon.

I do know that whatever they worship and its goal is a horror that, left unchecked, would destroy the minds and souls of the Crowned Kingdoms before long. This is most certainly the shrouded threat that Lanereth and Terra warned me about, and I can see why even their gods could provide little direction and clarity on the subject. This shade of a god seems to defy reason, perhaps even to the gods themselves.

I worry that the god Terra worships, the one and true Elendium, is not the god that rules over the church here in the kingdoms. It can't be. I've known the *power and spirit of Elendium before in my life—and the entity I contacted down there in that dungeon was most surely not him. Terra and Prophet Yunus may worship two separate gods—which is a horrifying thought given the sway the church of Elendium has in the Crowned Kingdoms.*

She cleaned the quill and placed it beside her journal, then leaned back, looking out the window that allowed her to see across the city that was lighting up now that dusk was setting in.

She found it helpful to journal when a lot was on her mind. It seemed to detangle things for her and clarify her focus—and right now, she desperately needed clarity. So much had happened after so little just days before. She wished that the universe would decide on a pace for her and stick with it but knew the idea to be folly as soon as she had thought it.

She had more to write about the trauma of the mind warp the Torchbearer in the cloister had unleashed upon her, but the pull of the spectacle of the lights below mesmerized her.

Perhaps she could afford to daydream on the wispy city, just for a few minutes more.

CHAPTER 10 - A SUDDEN TURN

It was early the next morning when Reza and Kaia were sent for. Neri and Jake had some trouble waking them, as both were exhausted from the last few days of non-stop travel and excitement. At length, they roused and were escorted to court.

Reza looked around the large courtroom, surprised at the welcoming setting the haltia had built for such a serious location. Most of their laws and judgments were handled here, yet the open archways all around the circular room opening up to terraces and balconies beyond added a pleasant touch to the white and green marbled room. The environment offered rest and comfort instead of judgment and sentencing. Even the birds playfully chirped and fluttered in and out of the hall's walkway around the room's perimeter.

The judge and his associates sat along a raised judge's bench, conversing amicably with each other as Reza and Kaia were guided to the speaker's stand.

General Seldrin entered the room and sat at a raised desk to the side of both them and the judges. With his arrival, chatter quieted at the bench, along with the few early birds in the public gallery.

Reza was on high alert, never having attended or studied the haltia court system. She figured that she would need to lean on Kaia for their defense more than she'd like. They couldn't afford a misstep here, and she didn't exactly have the best track record with courts and judges. She put the pain of her shoulder far to the back of her mind and attempted to focus on the line of haltia behind the raised stand.

The young, clean-shaven haltia judge stood and held up a hand for silence. He looked to Seldrin. "General Seldrin. Upon your request, we agreed to hold an expeditious case before the workday begins. Lay out the details of your request briefly so that we may proceed to seek a swift conclusion."

Seldrin bowed his head briefly, then turned his attention to Reza and Kaia, seated at the foot of the bench. "High Judge Astrin, these two were with the refugees that we brought before you yesterday. You know some of the details from my report already. These were the two females listed in the report that were clothed in White Cloak robes upon first contact. They claim reputable identities, however, and assert they're not associated with White Cloaks. Their case is convincing. I thought it prudent for the court to handle this case sooner rather than later due to their reputed status and ranking with some of our most valued allies. If they are who they claim to be, this case would merit a degree of priority so as not to burden them with undue delay in their objectives."

The young judge nodded and looked at the two

saren. "Your names, ladies?"

"Reza Malay, of the Southern Sands," Reza said.

"And Kaia Glading, of West Perch," Kaia added.

"They are both indeed allies to the Silver Crowns, West Perch especially. General Seldrin implied that you have titles or ranks associated with your respective territory? Lady Glading, why don't you go first? We are more familiar with West Perch."

"Certainly," Kaia said. "As you likely are aware, West Perch is the acknowledged authority and headquarters of the saren people for the continent of Darce. I am saren, as is Reza. I am a member of the intelligence board at West Perch and have been ordained as an official diplomat for my people."

"Very well," the judge acknowledged, looking then to Reza. "And you?"

Reza appreciated the judge's to-the-point pace. "I am a saren knight, originally stationed at High Cliffs Monastery in Jeenyre. The last few years, I was under Sultan Metus' command, of the Plainstate, and led several missions against an arisen force across various territories of the Southern Sands. I have official titles, but in general, I, along with my associates, were Sultan Metus' inner circle and personal strike force."

"Well, it does seem your accolades merit our early rising if you two are who you say you are. Is there any way for you to show us proof of your identity?

Anyone locally that would vouch for you personally? There is a small parish of Sareth here in Lancasteal. Perhaps they could consult records of your station if they keep such documentation."

Reza allowed Kaia to take lead on the question. "Yes, they may keep records there. My appointment was two years ago. As for immediate proof of my identity, I do carry the sign of Sareth," she offered, holding up the brooch with her symbol's faith emblazoned upon it.

The judge ordered her to approach the bench. She did so and allowed them a clear view of the brooch.

Satisfied, he looked to Reza. "And you, Knight Malay? What of your proof of office?"

"My tabard is my sign," she replied.

"Stand," he ordered. "Turn around so that we may see your emblem clearly."

She did so and showed the symbol of her order, worn and slightly faded but still recognizable. Golden angel wings housed a blood-red sword next to the golden orb of Lux, glowing with ghostly red flames about it.

"Indeed," the judge said. "The proof of identity is noted. It is sufficient enough to proceed with your account. Now then, why were you wearing White Cloak robes when General Seldrin came upon you?"

"We've heard rumors of people gone missing

around Rosewood and that the fledgling cult known as the White Cloaks had something to do with it. We had reason to believe those reports, so we launched an investigation of the location," Kaia answered.

"And was this an officially sanctioned initiative by West Perch?" the judge asked.

Kaia's hesitation prompted Reza to answer for them. "Not necessarily by West Perch, but by my commanding officer, High Priestess Lanereth at High Cliffs Monastery."

"But Rosewood would be more West Perch's jurisdiction than Jeenyre's, would it not?" the judge asked.

This time, Kaia answered. "Typically, yes, but due to our organization being a religious one and not a government, we have more interpretive flexibility on the topic of territories. A High Priestess may receive revelations not connected with her territory. Cross-territory revelation is not so uncommon in our faith. The saren's office trumps location-based administration as Sareth sees fit."

The judge seemed not to appreciate the answer, Reza noted, but Kaia's mixing of loose, spirit-of-the-law answers seemed to throw him off of that line of questioning.

"Very well. So then, you are saying that sarens are launching an official investigation on the White Cloaks' location at Rosewood, and by proxy, the church of Elendium, since that land belongs to the church?"

"I would not commit to saying that, exactly. We were concerned with the reports of missing persons associated with the location more than wishing to involve ourselves with the church of Elendium. Though, we've gathered reports across the kingdom of concerning volume about the presence of this White Cloak cult involved in suspicious operations."

"And what did your investigation involve, and what did you uncover?" the judge asked, though Reza noted he did so almost hesitantly.

Figuring she was best at giving mission briefs, Reza led the report. "We had been warned by locals not to approach the nunnery or risk being abducted, and so we decided to survey the location at night and to stay hidden."

"You trespassed," the judge said. His attendants took notes silently at his side.

Reza ignored the snag and continued. "We quickly came upon multiple human rights violations. The nuns' mouths were stitched together, we assume to force a vow of silence upon their worker worshipers. There was a holding room where twenty or more women of all ages were being held, naked, malnourished, bound, and abused. We freed that group. General Seldrin can attest to their state upon release that night."

General Seldrin nodded, and the judge prompted, "We've already had a report on the condition of the refugees, that won't be necessary. Is that the extent of your statement?"

"No," Reza replied, more than a little miffed with the judge's sudden lack of patience with the subject. "I witnessed a ceremony. A dark and strange one. I'm not sure how best to describe it, but they were worshiping a dark stone statue and mutilating the women down there, offering them up as sacrifices to their god, Umbraz. Kaia and I disguised ourselves in the robes of the White Cloaks to remain undetected. That was until I disrupted their ritual with the help of my friend, Nomad, who went missing afterward, leading pursuers away from myself, Kaia, and some of the would-be sacrifices. Upon escaping, we ran directly into General Seldrin at the crossroads. They captured us and brought us here for questioning."

Seeing that Reza's testimony was concluded, the judge asked Kaia, "Would you like to add anything else?"

Kaia nodded. "I agree with her account. I would also add that Rosewood is clearly violating multiple laws, by any kingdom's standards. Something needs to be done, and soon. I'm not sure we freed all the prisoners there. This needs to be made known to Alumin officials."

"And so it shall," the judge said. Kaia smiled at Reza. "The law is clear on the matter. You are to be delivered to Alumin for further questioning."

"What? Why?" both sarens asked.

"You do understand that Rosewood is not within our official territory, correct? Trespassing on church-owned property is grounds for a trial."

General Seldrin spoke up. "What law? This is the first I've heard of extradition for such a violation."

"Do you intend to represent the defendant?" the judge asked, turning on the general.

Seldrin was silent, taken aback.

The judge continued. "Any claims of human trafficking or violations of the law will be discussed further and at length in an Alumin courtroom."

Reza looked to the general, noticed his disappointment in the quick turn of sentence by the judge, then turned back to the board. "Surely you don't mean to extradite us to Alumin like criminals?"

"I am sympathetic to the hassle imposed upon you, but yes—the Silver Crowns has a strict policy involving Rosewood. Our hands are tied. Trespassing is an offense that must be answered for in Alumin. A rotating court is to see to all cases regarding Rosewood with Elendium representation present. It's a mandate by Alumin's rule of law, and our allyship depends on our upholding that agreement."

The judge's tone softened. "Don't worry. You'll be given a protected and comfortable transport to Alumin. General Seldrin will oversee your escort details. Take special care, general. Pick some of your most trusted officers to see to Miss Malay and Miss

Glading's journey. These are esteemed allies in our kingdom's care, after all."

The general recovered quickly from his bewilderment and replied firmly, "I will see that they make it safely there myself."

High Judge Astrin accepted Seldrin's assurance and held up a hand once more to announce the verdict had been made.

Reza and Kaia were escorted from the courtroom and returned to the care of Neri and Jake. The guards led them back to their rooms in silence, both saren still processing the sudden turn for the worse their hearing had taken.

"Might we room together this time? We've already had our hearing," Kaia asked Neri, who looked to Jake for comment.

"Sure. I don't see the harm in that," Jake replied. "One of us is still ordered to keep tabs on you, though."

Kaia went to retrieve her things from her room. Reza waited in the doorway as the two guards softly spoke to each other.

Jake turned to Neri and whispered, "I can tend to them today. Why don't you take the shift off? No sense in both of us sitting, watching in the hall on an uncomfortable stool."

"I'll keep you company if you don't mind. Besides, the general might be by at some point. I don't want to look like the lazy one," she said, smiling.

Kaia, arms full of her things, waited for Reza to lead her into her room.

"Sit tight in there. We'll give a knock and let you know when there's word on the itinerary for your escort to Alumin," Jake explained.

"Thank you," Kaia said with a smile, which got her a slight smile back from the two guards. They closed the door to allow Reza and Kaia privacy for the first time since they had been apprehended the day before.

"That did not go as I had hoped," Kaia said, placing her stuff down at Reza's bedside.

"No kidding." Reza flopped down on the bed and looked up at the ceiling.

"Being escorted back to Alumin isn't all that bad. Well, at least for me. That's where I needed to head to report the atrocities of Rosewood anyways. The board needs our report. Even if High Priestess Trensa doesn't care for you, they can't ignore this..." Kaia started, shaking her head. "But by the sounds of it, we're going to be the ones prosecuted, not the other way around. And the judge mentioned the rotating court and representation by the church of Elendium—that's not good."

"What's this rotating court? I've never heard of it," Reza said, looking at the pacing saren. She was starting to worry now that Kaia was working herself up.

"Well, it's a lower stand-in court. There's a joke amongst Alumin citizens that the rotating court is a mock court. It's a tool to prosecute unwanted cases and get undesirables out of the system quickly and quietly.

"How do they do that?" Reza asked. "Why is this court allowed?"

"I've only *heard* about the rotating court—never been to see a trial there. They don't assemble often and...well, I'm not exactly a legal expert. I've heard rumors that they even fill the seats with agents to keep the courtroom at capacity when they don't want the public to witness a case."

"Well, if that's where we're supposed to be tried, and the judge has already told us that there will be representation there from the church, I'm getting the feeling that we're headed for *trouble*, not help." Reza sat up to look out the window once more.

Her perspective on the lovely city of Lancasteal had been sullied quicker than even she had suspected it would.

CHAPTER 11 - SUPPRESSION

The morning sun began to filter through the trees, dewdrops on every leaf and cobweb glistening gold and white as Nomad rushed past. A flock of nesting birds flew off as the two crashed through the otherwise tranquil forest.

The hunchback was hot on Nomad's heels, even after a night of chase. A few times, Nomad swore he had seen the hulk phase in and out of space, tearing closer to him as he dashed and tumbled through the underbrush of the woods. He wondered if exhaustion was just catching up to him or if the hunchback's glowing scars were actually providing him some sort of supernatural speed.

Either way, the hunchback was not going to be shaken from his trail; that was certain at this point. Nomad needed to face the brute, and he had rather get the fight over with before he was completely spent. He was injured. His limbs were now only moving out of need. If he could take down the hunchback, he would stop to recover and assess the damage.

He loped into a clearing in the trees, the serene meadow juxtaposing against the struggle that was about to take place there.

He unsheathed his sword and turned to face the rampaging hunchback who was roaring now like a gorilla as he crashed into the opening. He slowed, seeing that his prey was no longer fleeing.

He paced about Nomad like a wild dog, ready to pounce at any moment. Nomad held his blade steady, point directed at the thing's head.

He had not had reason to use the blessing Bede had bestowed upon his ancestral blade for many seasons, but now, he sought to attune himself with the holy connection to her god as he once had done.

His curved sword began to glow—a dull white at first but growing in brightness as he readied himself to strike. He could only charge the blade for so long, he knew, already feeling what little energy he had left transferring into the searing hot edge.

For the first time, Nomad saw the hunchback give ground. The giant feared the holy glow.

He roared and snarled, baring his rotting teeth at the blade. He reflexively swatted at Nomad as he took a step forward. It was a mistake Nomad took advantage of, slicing cleanly through the large man's digits.

The hunchback erupted in yells of fury, doubling down on his attack, coming in and swinging wildly at Nomad.

Nomad had no spring left to attempt to dodge the flurry, instead placing his luck in a forward attack.

He slashed through the large man's arm, severing it at the shoulder and cutting back around to his torso.

The blade had cut through muscle and bone like a scythe through straw, but halfway through the brute's trunk, Nomad was slammed hard by his light-scarred arm.

Nomad tumbled head over heels across the meadow and crashed into a tree.

His eyes shot open in panic. He recalled instantly the mortal danger he was in from the hunchback. The giant's face was by his side, eyes wide in pain and anger.

Nomad, startled, crawled frantically back against the tree he had been knocked into but stilled after he realized he was staring at the hunchback's death mask. Half the man's torso was hanging open, and it looked as though the berserker had dragged himself across the forest floor, fatally wounded, to get to Nomad, but had died only inches away from reaching him.

He breathed, still eyeing the giant until he recovered enough to roll away.

His sword had been flung across the woodland clearing during the scuffle. As he moved to retrieve it, he gasped sharply, realizing that his hip was bound up, causing him to hobble stiffly.

Wincing in pain, he bent over to pick up his

sword and promptly sheathed his blade. He made it over to a tree to lean against and assess the situation, not knowing if he'd be able to get up again if he sat down.

He had no idea where he was, how badly he was hurt, where Reza and Kaia were, or if he was still being followed. He knew he was in bad shape.

He and the brute had run for hours—long after the other Torchbearers had given up the hunt. He could backtrack, or he could hope that he was close to an opening in the forest and attempt to get his bearings. For how far he had run that night, he figured the latter would be a better move.

Leaning against the tree, he took off his travel pack and started to search for a puck of ko hako to light up and kill the pain bleeding in, getting stronger by the second. If he didn't get ahead of the pain, he knew it could cripple him. He needed to force himself to keep moving.

He lit the incense and inhaled deeply, raising his eyebrows as a buzz ran through his sinuses. He continued to take in more smoke; already the ko was hazing the edges of his senses.

He packed up his travel pack, keeping the puck of incense lit in his hand. He snapped off a dead branch from the tree and broke it off on the other end to make a rough walking stick. Pushing off from the tree, he tested his balance.

He yelled out in pain as he attempted to hinge

his injured leg forward to hold his weight. It did, but hurt horribly. He gritted through a step, then another, arduously hobbling out of the clearing.

The day wore on as he slowly moved through the woods until sunset. He avoided resting, as he suspected his hip had been fractured, which he knew would only get worse over the next few days.

The sun had guided him west, the only direction he felt safe heading. To return south would mean certain doom. He was in no condition to avoid even a feeble Torchbearer's clutches at that point. If they came upon him now, he was theirs for the taking.

He only hoped that Reza and Kaia had taken advantage of his costly distraction and had gotten out of that horrid place.

He was in a fuzzy, dreamlike daze as he stumbled out of the forest's tree line. He looked out at the open plains that he hoped would lead to the highway back to Glensing.

He slumped against a tree and slid down it as his face contorted in excruciating pain. His leg, hip, and lower back were blistering hot, throbbing with every heartbeat.

He knew if he sat there then, he might not get back up for a very long time, if at all. Regardless of what his stubborn will wished him to do, his body had spent its last drop of reserves.

With a ragged heave, he collapsed into a

dead sleep, facing the golden plains of the Crowned Kingdoms as the sun set upon him.

CHAPTER 12 - REFLECTIONS

"Ho, ho," Seldrin called to his horse to hold up, tugging on the reins as they rode to a small cliffside that offered a view of miles of green meadows.

"Surely there's not a grander sight than from the grounds of Eden's Watch," Jake said with a smile as he rode up alongside the general.

"You're likely right, there," Neri agreed. She followed behind the two saren, who were speechless, taking in the impossible stretch of rolling hills that broke into miles of forests with grand, snow-capped mountains beyond.

"This is a sacred place—an old place," Seldrin said. "We will rest here for the night. It's been a long day."

They all dismounted and unpacked their gear while still freshly enchanted with the sweeping view of the Verdant Expanse that the cliffside plateau offered.

Reza followed the haltias onto the watchtower's grounds, taking note of where Seldrin and the others were stashing their things for the night. The tower's base was open and ancient, but the structure still appeared to be stable and safe to shelter under.

There were alcoves within. Seeing Jake and Neri taking an alcove together and Seldrin taking one all to himself, Reza nodded at Kaia to claim the last one for themselves.

Once they were out of city limits, Seldrin had given them back the remainder of their things as a token of trust. Reza felt that the general believed their story, and he'd shown them some degree of respect throughout their travels. She liked the man. However, since the hearing before the high judge, Seldrin had been more reserved and distant, allowing Jake and Neri to give most of the updates and orders through the day's travels.

"I'm going to watch the sunset," Reza announced. She headed out of the shelter back to the cliff's edge.

With the others milling about, setting up camp, and tending to the horses, she climbed down a section of cliff to lay out on a grassy ledge, desperately needing distance from everyone and everything.

She lay there for some time and watched the cream-tinted clouds float by as the sun crept closer to the horizon. The cliff's edge shielded her from the chill breeze that gusted over the lip of the turf above, which she was thankful for, as the temperature had already started to drop.

She sat up, looking out over the now shadowy meadow, thinking of Rosewood as she pulled the pearl necklace from her side pouch.

She began to study the trinket. She had seen a woman inexplicably turn into a pearl about the size of the one that was on this necklace. She hated to think that she held the remains of some poor girl from Rosewood.

It was an important artifact to those at the nunnery. She had not received insight into the items from her strange vision in the basement chapel, so she was left to speculate as she turned the bead over in her fingers.

A curious squirrel ventured down from the ledge Reza had scaled, its whiskers and nose twitching spastically. It noticed Reza and inched closer, its tail bristling with curiosity.

She fiddled with the pearl bead as she idly watched the critter observing her.

It squeaked, and Reza became aware of something wrong with the creature as it squirmed its head back and forth in agitation. Soon, the squeaks were more frantic, and it lost its hold on the rock and fell to the ground next to Reza, writhing in pain, locked in a desperate struggle for survival from an unseen threat.

Reza's focus shifted as her hand holding the pearl began to lock up, her fingers becoming cold and tingly. She tried to release it, but her fingers stuck to it as if glued.

She grunted with effort now. Finally, gripping her wrist, she wrenched her fingers free from the pearly bead and dropped it to the grass.

She eyed the pearl in disbelief, waiting to see if it would attach itself to her once more and continue to freeze the life from her, but it was still. The only sound now was the whistling wind as it whipped down off the cliffside overhead.

The squirrel that had made such a racket before was now quiet. She gasped as she looked to find only a clump of half-mutilated flesh, claw, and fur where the squirrel had been.

Images of Rosewood flashed in her mind, forcing her to grapple with the twisted warp she had both witnessed and endured some nights ago.

She took a sharp breath in and noticed a tear run down her cheek. She wiped it away and grunted as she banished the memory, looking back to the plain pearl. She thought about chucking it as far away from her as she could—then reconsidered.

Whatever the pearl was and whatever connection it had with the god Umbraz could clearly be used to do harm.

She unstrung her side pouch and snatched the necklace up, now terrified to touch the thing unprotected.

She held the pouch and stared at the mutilated squirrel for some time.

The sun had set. To avoid worrying the others of her whereabouts, she climbed back up the cliff, finding them loudly enjoying wine and brisket in the warmly lit ruins that sheltered them from the cold wind.

Kaia seemed happily engaged in conversation with Jake and Neri, the three generously sharing from the wine cask they had brought with them, while General Seldrin stood at the edge of the firelight, leaning on the doorframe of the interior of the watchtower.

He stepped into the shadows of the building out of her sight, and Reza followed.

"Reza, where have you been? I was starting to worry," Kaia asked, rosy-cheeked and smiling.

"Just…reflecting," Reza said.

"Come, eat and drink with us," Kaia offered, but Reza shook her head.

"I'm going to go talk with Seldrin." Reza passed by the merry crowd to peer into the dark of the tower's main room.

It took a moment for her eyes to adjust to the inner chamber. It smelled of dust and old wood, which threatened to make her sneeze a few times as she looked upward for signs of Seldrin. She spotted him just as he made his way out of sight near the old wood and stone stairs at the top of the tower.

She sighed, studying the old circular stairwell

steps a bit more before attempting the ascent. She started to follow after Seldrin, carefully stepping over the planks that looked rotten.

It had taken her a good five minutes to climb the steps where it had taken Seldrin only one. He knew the place though, and haltias were known to be extraordinarily light and nimble compared to other regional peoples. Even with her competitive nature, she dismissed the comparison as she clambered over the ledge and stood upon the watchtower's high lookout.

The wind was not as bad that high up, and though there were a few holes in the slate tile roof, it shielded them well enough from the rain that had started to drizzle down upon them.

Seldrin was watching the Verdant Expanse, near endless acreage of wilds devoid of any other signs of civilization. The land was shrouded in heavy clouds, the occasional moon ray showing silhouettes of forests and mountains far to the west.

"Dangerous climb," Seldrin said, still looking over the stretch of wilderness. "Even for a haltia."

"I've climbed worse," she stated matter-of-factly, walking over to join him at the banister.

"I'm sure you have," Seldrin said with a smirk.

He seemed to be reminded of something just then. As quickly as his smile had formed, it faded, and his gaze returned to the periwinkle clouds and glistening meadow far below.

"Something's...different about you since we had that hearing," Reza said, still looking over the man's features even as he looked away from her.

He didn't seem interested in responding, so she left him to his thoughts, gazing off into the cloudy vista along with him as the clouds slowly rolled by and dissipated into mist.

"I'm not happy with the judge's decision," Seldrin admitted suddenly. "I was hoping for them to see the need to stand against the church, and instead, you are being delivered to them."

"And you're the one delivering me to them," Reza added, though with no malice in her voice.

Seldrin sighed. "And I am the one delivering you."

Reza could understand Seldrin's distance from her and Kaia over the last few days. She had guessed about his coldness toward them—now it was confirmed.

She sat down, resting her back on the stone pillar supporting the old roof. The day had been a long one, and she was still sluggish from the night at Rosewood. Her shoulder had been healing well, but the recovery had sapped just enough energy from her to force her to rest throughout the day more than she would have usually needed to.

She must have looked beaten down and

exhausted. Seldrin sat next to her and rested a hand on her shoulder.

"I am sorry for your predicament," he whispered, watching the breeze pick up as it rustled the grassy plains. "I am mostly to blame for it, it seems."

She closed her eyes and breathed in the chill night air; the scent of wet lushness put her at ease.

"I suppose you were just tending to your duties..." she said at length and was going to leave it at that, but added after some thought, "...and still are."

This time it was Seldrin's turn to remain silent.

Wondering if he understood her meaning, she explained, "I don't appreciate that *we're* the ones to be tried. The church is clearly the one in question here, not Kaia and me. I don't like where you're taking us. I understand it's your duty to uphold your orders— but you know these orders aren't serving justice. It's serving a heel that your kingdom is under, be it public knowledge yet or not. It seems that the Silver Crowns justice system has bowed to the church of Elendium."

He had no response, and she wasn't able to read anything from his gaze overlooking the far-distant Jeenyre mountain range. She joined his search for answers out there amidst the moody night's vista, thinking over her time thus far in the Crowned Kingdoms and how little she had actually managed to accomplish there.

The mountain range looked foreign to her, especially at night, but she knew if she followed the foothills due west that she would eventually reach High Cliffs Monastery, her home—as much as she could call anywhere a home, at least.

Seldrin's eye and hand were plenty lenient —purposefully so, she figured. If she wished to, she knew that she could slip from their company and attempt to make her way back to High Cliffs and report on everything to Lanereth. *What would then come of Kaia and Nomad, though*, she thought. Regardless, it was not her nature to run from a fight.

"I just worry what will become of Kaia if we go before a corrupt court in her hometown. She's young, a good person as far as I've seen, and wants to make a real difference in the world. I can deal with a tarnished reputation in a foreign land. It would destroy *her*. She'd never be allowed back in West Perch.

"I've been too hard on her—and Nomad. I've been so frustrated over trying to make sense of what the church has been doing in the kingdoms that I've taken it out on them. I've been a miserable person, and worse, a miserable friend."

Another breeze blew through, carrying with it the clear hoot of an owl. Seldrin had listened to her self-assessment but left the remark alone as a sheet of rain rushed over the landscape, suddenly drowning out all other sounds.

It was some time before Reza stood to leave.

She felt a tad awkward over having shared her feelings with a man whom she had just met days earlier. It wasn't like her to do that, she reflected. But with Seldrin...she had an unspoken understanding with him, whether it was their common military background or his sensible approach in dealing with her. It was rare that she could trust a person so readily.

"Reza," he called as she started down the stairwell. She hesitated, though it was clear she wasn't going to wait long for him.

"Thanks for the company tonight," he said, his voice almost lost in the downpour.

Without a word, she disappeared into the dark.

The fire was low when she returned to the others. Neri and Jake were still conversing in low tones while Kaia snored softly by the fireside.

She hefted the girl, wincing as her shoulder twinged in pain, now inflamed from the difficult climb in the tower stairwell. She carried her over to the alcove where she had unpacked their stuff and laid her in the warm folds of her bedroll.

Reza watched her for a while, realizing the truth of her words to Seldrin earlier. She had been hard on the young saren, even harder on Nomad, and now one was missing, and the other was headed to a court system that seemed all but against them from the start.

She doubted that she would get much sleep

that night, and she was okay with that. She needed time to reflect on who she had become since leaving High Cliffs Monastery, and if possible—providing it wasn't too late—she needed to figure out how to make restitution with Kaia and Nomad.

CHAPTER 13 - ROAD TO ALUMIN

Reza toyed with the pearl necklace, mesmerized by it as it flickered in the sunlight. She was careful not to touch the pearl itself, dangling it by the leather cord from her hand.

During their ride over the last few days, she had given thought to its devastating potential. She knew what she had witnessed with the small squirrel. It had made quick work of the critter. She wondered if it was capable of wreaking the same havoc upon larger animals—or people.

She felt she knew the answer to that—not for certain, nothing was for certain regarding the cult of Umbraz, likely even amongst the devout followers themselves. She had seen the zealot that had warped her mind in the open cloister holding tight a pearl similar to the one she now had. She wondered…if she clutched the pearl and focused on Seldrin, Jake, and Neri…would there be anything they could do to stop her from doing to them what she had done to the squirrel? No longer would she and Kaia need to report to the court system in Alumin…. She shuddered even at the thought of such cruelty.

"Reza," Kaia called, riding closer to her.

Reza startled. "Y-yes?"

"You alright?" Kaia asked.

Reza carefully placed the necklace back in its pouch and cinched it up tight, nodding, attempting to also assure herself that she was alright.

"Um, Reza," Kaia asked. "There's something I need to discuss with you at some point."

"What is it?" Reza prompted.

"I've been reading from the church book we found at the Rosewood pulpit—" she started, struggling to put her thoughts into words on the subject. "It has some concerning...*messaging* about one called Umbraz. We should go over these findings once I've gone through it a bit more."

She had almost forgotten about the book Kaia had snatched up from the chapel that hectic night; she had pondered upon the discordant visions she experienced that same evening. She didn't doubt her cursed revelations of Umbraz would be reiterated or confirmed by the ravings found in that twisted chapel scripture.

She nodded. "That would be wise."

They rode in silence for a few moments. Reza looked over at the concerned, younger saren, thinking upon the girl in earnest. Kaia had stuck with her through the thick of it and displayed extraordinary courage the night of the Rosewood operation, especially for never having been in such a hostile situation before.

"Thank you, Kaia," Reza said. She reached out to hold Kaia's hand. "I—haven't treated you with as much respect as I now know I should have. You've been good to me and Nomad, and you show promise as a priestess of Sareth."

Reza let Kaia's fingers slip from hers. They nudged their horses along once more, Kaia smiling shyly now, a bit taken aback by Reza's unusual display. It was clear Kaia didn't know what to say, and so the two rode a few more miles in comfortable quiet, the chill breeze gusting through the group as they came to the bridge crossing.

"On watch," Seldrin called from the front, turning in his saddle to address Reza and Kaia. "There's a reason I wished to come this way."

Reza trotted to catch up.

"See that tree line to the east?" he asked, eyeing a woodland area along the riverbank that stretched for miles.

Reza nodded.

"Well, we've gotten reports of bandits camping in those woods. They've hit the highway across the river several times over the last year. Too sporadic for Alumin or Rediron to do anything about it. Technically, where they've been hitting isn't in Silver Crowns, but they might squat on our borders. Haven't gotten a report for a few months now, but...you never know. Best to keep on guard. If they do try something, have your weapons ready and stay close."

Reza nodded again and fell back to trot next to Kaia. If any needed protection in the company, it would be her.

The ride up to the bridge was quiet and tense; all were on high alert, focused on their surroundings more than conversing with each other as they had earlier in the day.

For Reza, the mood was refreshing. Her mind felt at home when engaged in searching for hidden threats. Through the years, she had taught herself to maintain a constant focus on her peripheral. Her situational alertness was honed. She hadn't needed that skill as much in the past few months, and since Rosewood, she was beginning to feel the charge of tapping that skillset once more.

The horses' hooves clopped over the wooden bridge; everyone was painfully aware of the noise they were making as they traversed.

The gurgling river drowned out any other sounds, causing Seldrin to raise his voice to be heard. "At attention!" he called, eyeing two riders from the east.

It was a matter of minutes before they met the two riders at the crossroad that forked to Canopy Glen and Alumin.

"Good eve," Seldrin hailed, keeping his company

tight behind him as the two rode up.

"Evening," one of the riders called back with a smile. "Y'all from Silver Crowns?"

"Indeed we are."

"Military?" the other rider jumped in. "I've seen Silver soldiers up this way once before. Your tabards look the same."

"Aye," Seldrin replied. "And yourselves?"

"Canopy Glen detachment. Road Rangers patrolling the highway from here to Alumin."

"Good to hear. I've gotten reports of highway bandits around these parts. Nice to see Rediron's presence along these roads."

"Ah, yes, those ruffians were an issue for a while there," the ranger gruffed back. "From what I've gleaned, they were some growers attacking on the highway to make ends meet. Reports have died down recently, though. Ever since the warp threw our kingdom into a tailspin and we kicked those White Cloaks out of our lands. Everyone here's had their hands full, I think, including those junkies. Anyhow, we've been out patrolling more since the new king started governing."

"New king?"

"Yeah, Marshal Reid stepped up after the king's assassination a week ago," the other ranger finished for his partner.

"Assassination?" Seldrin asked. "We've not heard word of that in Silver Crowns."

The first rider sighed and nodded. "There's been a few public audiences, but it's been a hectic time for all the officials. Things seem to be on the up and up, though. Marshal Reid is quite respected by the people, including lords, army, and citizenry. As I understand it, he's rolling out some real plans to get to the bottom of the cause and cure for the warp sickness."

"The warp, yes," Seldrin said, rubbing his chin. "I've heard that Rediron has been struggling with that plague for the last year now. Strange how it only affects Rediron towns. I wonder if it's something in the water."

"You make a solid case there. Never thought of it that way, but you're right. We've not seen other kingdoms suffer as our kingdom has from that sickness. Though, I've heard Alumin is having some troubles all their own recently, maybe worse than us Redironers."

"Like what?" Seldrin asked. "What could possibly be worse than the warp?

"More visitors from Alumin are heading down our way this last week," the other ranger cut in. "That's why Reid has ordered more Road Rangers to patrol it. Something up there ain't sitting right with the city folk. Too many Elendium followers been migrating there. People aren't happy with that."

"Surely that's of lesser concern than being

ravaged by the warp," Reza interjected.

"Apparently not for those coming here from Alumin," the lead ranger said with a shrug. "What's that saying? *Leaving one devil to be tormented by another*? Sometimes it seems like anything is better than what you've been dealing with, even if all you're doing is *trading devils*. Hell, I thought about packing up more than a few times with all this warp sickness going around. Downright insufferable watching my homeland go to shit right before me eyes. Maybe those folk up in Alumin are feeling the same way, but where's there to go that don't have its fair share of problems...?"

"Thanks for the heads up," Seldrin said after the ranger's last question lingered unanswered.

"No problem," both rangers said in unison.

The lead ranger turned his horse to go. "Keep your eyes peeled up north. Can't be too careful these days, what with White Cloaks popping up everywhere."

Seldrin nodded and thanked the ranger once more before spurring his horse east along the highway toward Alumin. Reza and the others followed.

It was a few minutes before Seldrin pulled back to talk in private with Jake and Neri. Then he fell back to Reza and Kaia to announce that they'd be finding shelter along the forest's edge within the next hour of travel.

They passed a few caravans, all heading south toward Canopy Glen, which confirmed the ranger's claim that a movement was in force. None of the travelers seemed as though they wished to stop to chat as the rangers had. Seldrin, Neri, and Jake were preoccupied with finding a place to set up camp regardless, and before the sun had fallen too far below the horizon, they had picked a spot Reza recognized. She'd stopped there with Nomad some weeks earlier in their trip to Alumin.

Dinner that night was served and eaten in silence. Not even Jake and Neri roused a conversation amongst the group as they had previous nights, and Reza thought she knew why.

They were nearing Alumin. That night was likely their last under the stars on the trail. Tomorrow, they would arrive for processing and be delivered to the courts and into the clutches of the church. She was sure each had their own reasons to dread what awaited them in the capital.

Though the last few nights Reza had stayed up talking with Seldrin, she decided to turn in the same time as Kaia that night. The two went to bed down a small way off from Seldrin and the others.

"Kaia," Reza whispered into the dark as Kaia finished settling into her bedroll. "I don't know what's going to become of us after our hearing, but if any of this jeopardizes your standing with West Perch and you're turned away from the sisterhood, I just wanted to let you know, I'll make sure that you'll have a place at High Cliffs Monastery. Lanereth is strict, but she's fair, and she'd take you in—"

"If they exile me from West Perch, I don't think another convent would be my first choice for relocation. I'd rather follow you, Reza, *actually out there,* making a difference in the world," Kaia whispered.

"I don't know if I'm making a difference," Reza protested, "but...you're welcome to accompany me wherever the trail leads—if we can *find* the trail after tomorrow's hearing, that is."

There was silence at the grim thought, as each wondered about the eventful day ahead of them.

"Thanks, Reza," Kaia whispered, leaning over to embrace Reza.

Reza smiled in the dark, looking up at the stars, and let out a peaceful breath.

"Thank you, dear," she whispered back, squeezing Kaia's hand once before letting her go.

The two watched the stars drift in the night sky for a bit longer before falling asleep.

CHAPTER 14 - FAMILIAR FACES

They had made good time that morning; the road headed toward Alumin was busy, but nothing impeded their pace. They were allowed within city limits with no holdup by the guards who were preoccupied with handling outbound traffic.

Reza and Kaia could both feel a different energy since they left Alumin just a week earlier. Seldrin had not allowed for a stop on their journey, thinking it best to make it to the capitol building first to gather intel from more reputable sources rather than poll random passersby on what all the commotion was about.

Seldrin's credentials were impeccable, each checkpoint within the judicial district allowing them to pass with only a few words from the general. It was clear he was known in the city, and once inside the grand capitol building that crafted, enforced, and interpreted law upheld by all surrounding kingdoms, he had been directed quickly to the clerk that processed cases such as Reza's.

"General Seldrin, correct?" a spectacled man behind a clean marbled desk asked.

"Just so," Seldrin confirmed.

As the judicial clerk thumbed through some papers, a white-robed man took note of the group and approached, standing behind the counter next to the clerk. Reza and Kaia recognized the man immediately, and by the way he returned their gaze, it was apparent that he recognized them. It was the faith worker from the synagogue who had found them in the inn and then took Reza to see Prophet Yunus —only now he wore White Cloak robes instead of Elendium's traditional red and gold colors. His thin-framed, circular spectacles only seemed to narrow his squinting gaze further as he peered at Reza.

The clerk looked up, took note of the White Cloak's presence, and then went back to find the file he had been searching for.

"Ah, yes, the attendants told me you were seeking an inquiry about some prosecution. This isn't a small claim, correct? You wouldn't be here if it were, I suppose. Are these the accused?" the man asked, looking at Reza and Kaia.

"Yes," Seldrin said.

"Well, you can hand them over now if you wish. I'll send for an Alumin security detail and hold them until their hearing time," the clerk suggested. "Or you can see them to the lobby of the church yourself."

"The church? What about the court?" Seldrin asked, his impatience rising.

"All legal cases are temporarily being held at the church of Elendium until further notice," the clerk replied, as though it was not the first time he had said the line that day.

Seldrin attempted to keep his calm, though it was clear to everyone that his patience was wearing thin. "Why?" he asked.

The clerk sighed. "Orders from the governor-general himself."

"That didn't answer my question."

"The judges have no complaints with it, so that means neither do we," the clerk said, side-eyeing the faith worker who watched them like a bird of prey. "You can ask them yourself before or after the hearing if you're that curious—if they have the time to chat on their break. Things have been quite busy this week with all the fuss over the relocation."

"Alright," Seldrin gave in, moving on from the subject that was becoming an argument. "What's the docket look like? When can we expect to be seen?"

"For a general, they'll make time to see you today," the clerk said, relieved that the general was asking easier questions. "Someone at the church's lobby will assist you."

"I will see to this personally," the faith worker interjected, with no room for leeway in his voice.

Seldrin idled at the clerk's desk for a moment, thinking over the strange changes to the Alumin court system since last he visited.

"Meet us there, then. I'll see to their arrival. You can take it from there," Seldrin said, clenching a fist and stepping away before the faith worker could protest the decision.

As they turned to go, Reza and Kaia watched the White Cloak, who glared back at them, leaving them with dread deep in their stomachs.

They had been directed to report to the Elendium synagogue, a direction that was at once a shocker to everyone in the company while at the same time confirming their worst suspicions.

They headed out of the judicial district and were starting toward the church when Seldrin's pace began to flag. He soon thereafter halted them to the side of a smaller, empty street.

He turned to speak quietly with Jake and Neri, eyeing the two saren. At length, he stepped up to Reza and Kaia and addressed them.

"Reza, I don't know what game the Alumin leadership is playing at here, but something's... amiss," Seldrin started. He looked to Kaia. "You're from here. Have you noticed anything different?"

"We've only stopped at the capitol building. I can't really say." Seeing that he wasn't satisfied with the answer, she offered, "It does seem like there's more traffic leaving town than usual."

"Something's not right," he grumbled, looking

across to the busier part of town. "I didn't like my orders to begin with. It was clear to me you and Kaia were not at fault for the Rosewood incident, but Judge Astrin insisted you be deported for a trial here."

Reza held her hopes in reserve. Seldrin had seemed to side with them from the start, but she needed confirmation of a decision before getting her hopes too high. "What are you getting at?"

"I don't think you should be here, and I don't intend to force you to stand before a church-run court whose biases would surely condemn you and cover up any actual misdeeds occurring in Rosewood. There's no justice in that course—and I don't plan to enable it, even if it comes with severe repercussions."

Kaia turned to Reza, wearing a wide smile over the sudden news, but Reza held her composure. "You mean to let us go, here and now?" she asked.

"Yes—I'm releasing you from Silver Crowns custody effective immediately," Seldrin said with a perfunctory wave of the hand.

Reza finally returned Kaia's smile and accepted the girl's giddy embrace.

"I have hopes, though, that our ways might not part immediately, Reza Malay," Seldrin interrupted. The two saren settled down as he continued. "I might very well be trading in my general's crown for this act of insubordination. I figure that's at least enough to earn me a drink with you. I do still have questions I've been meaning to ask—if that's alright with you."

Seldrin smiled. Reza had rarely seen warmth from the man, at least openly. She couldn't deny that the gesture warmed her.

"A saint and a gentleman, not common qualities for military leaders where I come from." The comment came from a man leaning against the building on the street corner, flipping a dagger expertly over and over in his hand.

"Sareth save us," Reza exclaimed, recognizing the voice. It was her long-time comrade, Fin, who sheathed his dagger deftly before approaching them.

"Fin, how did you—" Reza breathed, lost for words at the unexpected sight of the man.

"After two days of James' constant yammering, I found myself off on the trail to find you. Damned sure wasn't going to sit around that farm another month waiting for you to finish up here in Alumin. Forgot how antsy I get when there's waiting involved," Fin explained, clapping Reza on the back and embracing her.

"Good to see you again, ol' girl," he sighed.

She hugged him tight, realizing just then how badly she needed an embrace from an old friend.

"Who is this?" Seldrin asked.

It was Kaia who answered as Reza composed herself. "Are you Fin, the famed picaro of the Southern Sands?"

Fin gave the young saren a surprised, warning

look, but that only prompted her to expound. "I've read that you helped Reza in the war against the arisen. You are said to be an expert knifeman—unless I'm mistaking you for someone else?"

"A picaro, eh?" he mused. "Well, that description of me is kinder than I typically am given."

"So you *are* him?"

"Yes, girl. Quiet down with your proclamations —" he said, but was cut off by Reza squeezing him tight one more time.

He flinched and eased her away. Answering her questioning look, he whispered, "Easy. Got a bit banged up in Rediron. Still on the recovery."

Seldrin's haltia ears perked up. "What were you doing in Rediron?" he asked. Seldrin hadn't taken his eyes off Fin since he had shown up, a fact that Fin had taken notice of.

"Great, another haltia to deal with," he breathed. Turning to Reza, he asked, "From what I overheard, you seemed...you're not actually with this guy, are you Reza? What did you get tangled up in while we've been apart?"

"He's...well...it's complicated," she said, looking to the general. "Seldrin, do you mind giving us time to catch up? I'll take you up on a drink and a chat later this evening, just—I need time to catch up with Fin first. Meet me at the pub, Dolingers, on the west side of town at sundown. We'll talk more then."

Seldrin looked displeased with the arrangement, and though he didn't protest, he watched as Fin led Reza off. Kaia followed after the pair into the bustling streets.

CHAPTER 15 - A TIMELY REUNION

Fin pinched the bridge of his nose, sighing heavily. He took a seat across from Reza at the circular table in the den of a small rental house he had been staying at.

"What the hell's been happening up here, Reza?" he huffed. "A coup upon the capital city of a nation, you've apparently been held captive by a general—who for sure has a thing for you, and Nomad met the wrong side of a giant."

"How do you know about Nomad? Do you know where he is?" Reza entreated, suddenly frantic.

Fin took a moment to reset and lowered his voice. "He's resting in a room down the hall."

He gripped Reza's arm hard as she moved to stand up. "*He's resting*, Reza. He's pretty banged up, in a lot of pain when he's awake. Let him rest for now."

Reza had a thousand questions. Her mind was ablaze with so many conflicting emotions that she struggled to decide where to begin.

"I know you hate healings," Fin started for her, "but Nomad might require one if you're up to it."

Reza stilled. She had had a rough history with

her kind's ability to mend wounds. She knew few other saren who were as terrible as she was at it, and she had shied away from using her gift except under the direst of circumstances. In all truth, she was frightened of it. If she did not control the flow of life energy precisely during a healing, she could transfer too much to the patient and inflict irreparable damage on herself, or worse, give her life up completely in the effort. Healings had a way of running away from a saren's control without complete focus.

"I could help," Kaia said from the corner. "I'm a priestess. I've studied healings since…well, as long as I can remember."

Reza thought about Kaia's offer for a moment. Nomad was, first and foremost, *her* friend and *her* responsibility, not Kaia's. However, she knew he would be better tended to by most any other saren when it came to a healing. Against her internal mulish objections, she forced herself to accept the offer. "I'll aid you during the healing," she softly agreed.

"Good," Fin said, clasping his hands together. "*Thank Sareth*, the man needs it—but as I said, he's sleeping, and while he is, you've got a lot of explaining to do. Nomad told me about Rosewood. He distracted the host while you escaped. Reza, why didn't you return for him?"

The question stung worse than she thought it would. She teared up. It was a question she had asked herself every day since they had parted ways. She hated herself for not finding a way to make it back to search for him.

"There, there," Fin whispered gently, only seeing now how torn up Reza was over the subject.

She shrugged his comforting hand from her shoulder, then cupped her hands to her face. Hot tears were streaming down from her eyes whether she wished them to or not.

Fin softened his tone considerably. "That was a dumb question. I'm sorry. It was clear you were being detained by that general fellow. You would have returned for Nomad if you could have."

"Bastard," Reza grumbled in an unsteady voice.

"That's probably a better descriptor of me than a damned picaro," he said with a sheepish grin.

She couldn't help but chuckle through a sob. She shoved him halfheartedly, grumbling, "Damn it, Fin." She sobered up as best she could, wiping her tears away. "I did try to return for him. I did—"

She stared down at the table, thinking back upon the last week of their travels. "I just couldn't find an escape—until now. But...I was...that's just not good enough."

The silence in the room accentuated the statement. Reza whispered aloud, "*I'm* just not good enough."

"Enough," Fin admonished, drawing her eyes to his. "It's not too late for Nomad. Sure, he's seen better days, but with a saren's touch, we'll have him back on his feet in no time. He'll be fine."

Fin placed a hand on Reza's knee. This time, she accepted the gesture.

"Besides, if you want something to worry over, worry about the Crowned Kingdoms," he added, weight returning to his voice.

She looked at him questioningly.

"Do you know what day it is?" he asked.

"No idea," she admitted.

"It's Thursday," he explained, sitting back in his chair. "On Sunday, Alumin sent proclamations throughout the capital declaring new laws set to go forth immediately—no citizen vote, means of recourse, nothin'. On Monday, the law was codified and distributed via treaties posted in every square and church."

He let the news sink in as he poured himself a drink of wine. "Tuesday, White Cloak missionaries were out en masse, proselytizing. Wednesday marked the first church trials—it's practically a church-run state at this point."

He poured another drink and handed it over to Reza, figuring she would need it. "Today, the people of Alumin organized and held their first protest. I've gotten word that protests are only the beginning. A riot is brewing, and things are going to turn plenty ugly when that happens."

Reza held the clay mug in her hand, taking it all in. "Fin, how long have you been in Alumin?"

"Couple of days, I suppose. Hasn't been more than a week."

"How do you know all of this? How did you find Nomad for that matter?"

"Info and manhunting are my trade, love. I'm good at it," he replied. Leaning in, he added as an afterthought, "You know, sometimes I think you forget that you're surrounded by some pretty amazing friends with a lot of valuable talents—and I'm not just talking about myself. Each of our mates brings to the table an invaluable skill set. You'd do well to rely upon others a bit more instead of trying to carry the world's burdens upon your shoulders."

She took a sip of the wine, then looked at herself in the liquid's deep-red reflection. "Yes, you all *are* amazing. It's *me* who keeps coming up short."

"That's hardly true," Fin said, leaning in. "You have the most valuable talent of us all. Without you, there would be no *us*."

"And what is that?" she asked, self-loathing still tinging her voice but with some hope mingled in.

"Commitment, determination, drive—perhaps it's something along those lines. A simple word would fall short of defining the undying spark that you possess. Without you, all of Southern Sands would have fallen. No one else would have held on to hope to see us through the rigors of that war. No one else had hope of even attempting to stand up and fight against Sha'oul. Not Lanereth, Sultan Metus, any of the war leaders, or even your closest comrades—not without you there leading the charge, that is."

She was frozen in place at her friend's assessment of her grit. Fin continued. "You're stubborn as hell, and I know that creates problems for you and those around you at times, but that's what gives you the power to press forward through all the bullshit of others telling you *no*, or that *it can't be done*. You're the strongest person I know, Reza. Never doubt how special a soul you are. I'll always believe in you, and I'm always going to be there for you. You're the closest thing I've ever had to a sister. You and Cavok, you're my mates for life."

She tried to hold back a fresh flow of tears but couldn't stop herself from breaking down. Fin came over to her, and she readily accepted the embrace, not even caring at that point that Kaia was there to witness the rare moment of vulnerability.

She allowed herself a minute to sob, releasing all the pent-up emotions that she had been struggling with alone for so long, thankful for the support of her longtime, faithful friend; then, patting him on the back, she whispered in his ear, "So glad you're here, Fin. I needed you. *We* needed you."

"Glad I got here when I did," Fin whispered back.

He let her go, and she settled back into her chair.

"Where's Yozo?" she asked.

Fin sighed, attempting to figure out how to put things simply so as not to take the rest of the afternoon from her. "Well, last I saw him, he was doing just fine—much better than me and Mal—"

"You found Malagar?" Reza interrupted, excited to hear about the success in finding their missing companion.

"Yes..." Fin admitted. "We did, but...well, I'm not going to sugarcoat it. Mal was tortured—horribly so, I'm afraid to say. We busted him out of that asylum, but he's likely never going to recover from what they put him through in there, even if Yozo made it back to High Cliffs Monastery in time to have Lanereth tend to his wounds. The mental scars he's going to carry with him from his stay at the abbey may fade with time, but...I just can't see a path to a full psychological recovery."

Reza was crestfallen by the news. She hadn't known the haltia Malagar other than what others had said of him, but she knew how much he had meant to Fin, Yozo, and Lanereth specifically. To hear such an awful fate had befallen the man tore at her sympathies.

"Lanereth will see him fully healed, of that, I'm certain," Reza offered, seeing how affected Fin was over the matter.

"She will," he agreed, clearing his throat. "We did more than just save Mal, though—and this part involves you and what's been happening up here in the other kingdoms—"

He paused, looking over to Kaia sitting at the far end of the otherwise empty den of the private rental home, attempting to keep out of the way. He waved her over.

"Kaia, was it? Pull up a chair. You're freaking me out over there in the shadows," Fin called out. "If Reza approves of you, you're all in, in my books—unless you don't wish to be party to our crew's actions and schemes, in which case, please pack up and leave. I'm about to dive deep into some sensitive subjects."

"I'm all in," Kaia said quietly, holding the Rosewood scripture against her chest as she pulled up a chair to the table.

"Atta girl," he said approvingly, giving her a wink before returning Reza's gaze. "This White Cloaks cult, it's no joke. They almost had both the Rediron and Black Steel kingdoms in one clean sweep. Yozo and I foiled it, though. Mucked it up real good. I left it all in the hands of a marshal by the name of Reid down there. Seemed like a decent enough guy, more level-headed than any other option at the time. Anyways, we didn't have much choice—"

"Reid?" Kaia asked, recalling the name from the day before. "That's the new king, is it not? After the last one was assassinated."

Reza gasped. "Fin, you didn't…did you?"

"Had no choice," he stated. "The damned maniac was in league with the cult of Umbraz. He was actively poisoning his own people and handing the remains over to Black Steel's Mad Queen. He had to be stopped."

"Regicide..." Reza breathed, a little lightheaded even at the sound of the word.

"I came up here soon after," Fin said, taking another drink of his wine to allow the heavy mood to clear. "I started gathering intel, mostly seeking you two out. Finding Nomad was easy. He's even more a foreigner than us Southern Sand folk. Got word that there was a strange foreign man found roadside near Glensing. I was at his bedside that evening and brought him back to Alumin. He caught me up on your situation prior to Rosewood. Sounds like you two really kicked the wasps' nest."

"I suppose we did do that," Reza agreed.

"Well, the next day, once Nomad was boarded and taken care of, I set out to investigate what all the fuss was about amongst the locals. That was Sunday. Everyone was up in arms over some decree. I, uh..."

"*Uh*, what?" Reza asked. If Fin himself was showing worry over his actions, she certainly should be worried, if not panicked.

"Well, I fell in with a rowdy group of fellows. They typically have the loosest lips and access to info. I found out that they were part of a long-standing resistance movement. Call themselves the Kingsmen.

They have a loose network throughout most of the Crowned Kingdoms. They've been busy tracking the moves of the Umbraz cult from the start, mostly because that's what led to the *Lost King* becoming *lost* in the first place. He was the cult's first target, apparently. So these loyalists have been stirring up trouble where they can and selectively recruiting. I'm accepted by the local gang here, but I'd like to talk with the Lost King himself, assess whether we can trust and partner with this high-asset ally."

"That makes sense," Reza nodded, impressed by the amount of legwork Fin had run through in such a short time. "We can talk more about our plans going forward later. You mentioned you were injured," she said. "Let me see it."

"I'm fine. You need to save that saren magic of yours for Nomad," he said, waving away her concerns.

"Fin..."

He gave her a look, knowing now that if she was focused on his injury, she wasn't going to stop pestering him about it until she got a look at the gash in his gut.

He stood and lifted his blood-speckled undershirt to reveal a still healing stomach wound.

Reza gasped, and Kaia exclaimed, "Oh gods! You need medical attention immediately!"

"It's not that bad, I swear. I stitched it up myself!"

"That's exactly what it looks like, and that's why it worries me," Reza murmured. "Good god, Fin. How did you travel all the way to Alumin in that state?

"I actually caravanned here, so I didn't do much walking till I got to Alumin. It has been weeping more the last few days, though..."

"Do you think you can handle a double healing if I support you?" Reza asked Kaia.

"I will do what I can," Kaia said. "First, we need to see the condition of your other friend. At the least we can stabilize them both and deal with further care over the next few days as our energy returns to us."

"Tend to Nomad first," Fin demanded. "If you two still feel up to touching me up a bit, I'll accept the blessing—*but* I don't want you depleting yourselves over me. I've been doing fine up till now and can hang on a few more days if you need to rest."

The two saren did not immediately agree to his terms.

"Hey, don't wipe yourself out for us, okay?" Fin said, then looked to Kaia. "Neither of ya."

"I need to see him, Fin," Reza said, and in her voice was the tender worry of a friend.

Fin looked at Reza, seeing depths of pain—of regret.

"Sure, I'll take you to him," he grunted, clearing his throat, and added with a bit of forced chipperness, "We can't have him sleeping all day, now, can we?"

Smiling, Reza got up and hugged Fin once more, gently in respect for his injury.

She whispered in his ear, "I'm glad you're here, Fin."

Fin smiled and put a reassuring arm around her once more.

CHAPTER 16 - ON THE RUN

The door to a small, dark bedroom cracked open.

"Nomad," Fin said softly, looking in first to make sure he was presentable before allowing Reza and Kaia in.

Fin called again, this time louder. Nomad groaned as he awoke.

"Hand me that candle," Fin ordered Kaia.

Taking the light, he looked over his friend and saw that he was awake, just reluctant to respond. Nomad held his hands over his eyes, either to ward off the intruding light, or to concentrate on controlling the pain.

"Nomad," Fin called. "I've found Reza. Brought her here to give you a blessing."

"Reza—" Nomad croaked. He finally lowered his hands from his eyes and Reza could see that he had been in tears for some time.

"Nomad—" she whispered tenderly, kneeling down next to him and holding one of his hands in hers. "I'm so sorry we couldn't come back for you. *I'm sorry—*"

Nomad issued a sharp gasp of pain, pausing Reza mid-sentence.

"Fin, where's he hurt? What's wrong with him?" Reza asked, looking back to see Fin's somber visage.

"He told me that a giant smashed his hip," Fin sighed. "I was able to score some drugs to help with the pain, but it's gotten worse. I was out today trying to find a doctor that takes house calls. Found you instead."

"Fin, drugs aren't going to help mend a broken pelvis."

"I'm not a doctor, Reza—" Fin cut back, then collected himself. "I was doing the best I could, but there's a reason I was never the one tending to everyone's injuries. You and Bede were the healers, not me."

"You're right. I'm sorry, Fin," Reza admitted, standing to pat Fin on the side. "You found him and us, and that's what matters. We'll take it from here."

"I'm ready when you are, Reza," Kaia prompted. She unclipped her faith's brooch and held it reverently in her palm.

"Alright." Reza placed a hand upon Kaia's back and chest to envelop her core.

Although she had shadow healed before, acting as a second for the primary healer, it always set her on edge. With Kaia performing the actual workload of the blessing, Reza only needed to provide her with access to her own lifeforce. Even to do that was still a feat that required extreme concentration.

She focused now on opening her spirit pathway to Kaia's. As Kaia began to lay her hands upon Nomad's chest, Reza also felt Kaia's spirit reach out and touch hers as energy began to drain from her.

Reza noticed that Kaia, for all her youth, was transferring energy at a very steady rate. She calmed her nerves slightly and turned full control over to the gifted saren priestess.

Kaia slowly increased the tug on Reza's lifeforce. Reza knew that Kaia was deep into the injury reconstruction process.

A bang at the front door startled them, disrupting the blessing. There was another loud, impatient rap at the door. Fin left the room to go investigate, but the interruption had put a pause on the healing as Kaia lifted her hand from Nomad's chest with some effort. Reza caught Kaia as she swayed in place.

"You alright?" Reza asked, looking down to see the girl's eyelids flutter for a moment before she shook her head, gathering herself.

"Y-yeah. I'm okay," she said, looking toward the door. "What was that? Where's Fin?"

Reza listened intently now. The front door opened, then she heard Fin's voice low down the hallway, then the reply of another voice.

"Someone's at the door," Reza whispered.

"Reza," Nomad said, sitting up, looking a great deal better than only minutes ago. "What's happening?"

"We have word that there's a defiler being harbored here," the voice at the door said.

Tensions were escalating. Fin started to raise his voice in return. The three in the back room knew they needed to act fast.

"I don't know," Reza admitted. "But we need to leave here right now. Can you walk?"

"You'll be tried for harboring enemies of the church if you don't let us in this house right now!" a man yelled shrilly.

Nomad went to stand up, wincing once his feet touched the floor planks, but stood up on his own, testing himself as he walked over to throw on his travel pack.

A yell came from the front door, a short scuffle, then a resounding slam. Footsteps rushed toward them, and Fin appeared in the hallway.

"We've got to go, now," he whispered, violent pounding on the front door punctuating his point.

He snatched up his pack of belongings, then went to support Nomad, nudging his arm under Nomad's shoulder, and started toward the back door. Reza and Kaia rushed after him as the slamming on the front door threatened to breach at any moment.

"Here," Fin called back, holding open the back door as Reza and Kaia rushed out of the house.

Kaia took a fall off the back porch, landing hard on the grassy lawn. At first, Reza had thought she had tripped, but as Kaia struggled to get back up, she realized that Kaia was probably exhausted from the healing. She scooped her up, looping her arm over her shoulder just as Fin had done with Nomad. Fin paused to make sure the two were alright, then they rushed from the yard.

Even though they were nearly into the next property over, they could hear the splintering explosion of the front door as the intruders broke through and entered the house.

Fin was weaving through yard after yard, looking back to make sure the others were following him. He only stopped after they rounded an alleyway that blocked them from view of his rental.

"Men from the church," Fin said, mostly to Reza, as the other two were so winded and struggling that he doubted they were in a state to consider his words. "You're on their list, Reza. They knew you by name. They're looking for you. I assaulted them. We're all on the run now."

They could hear shouting coming from the rental property now, and the first pattering of rain began to pelt down upon them.

Reza could see Fin was lost in thought, but as another yell, closer this time, sounded from the church ruffians, she spoke her mind. "I need to get back to Dolingers—"

"No," Fin cut her off. "We need to connect with my contacts and get passage to the Lost King. We need to get out of this town now that we're targets of the church. It might even lend us additional credibility with the Kingsmen."

"Fin, I need to talk with Seldrin," Reza demanded. Fin could tell that she was not going to budge on the decision.

The church ruffians were spreading out now, calling from yard to yard, getting closer. Fin knew there was no time left.

"I'll take Nomad and contact the Kingsmen. I'll meet you at Dolingers. We'll skip town from there. Sound like a plan?"

Reza nodded, and the two started off, practically carrying their injured friends down the alley and into a street leading away from the searchers. A sheet of heavy rain washed over them, covering their escape.

CHAPTER 17 - LEAVING TOWN

The rain was heavy, with no signs of lightening up by the time Reza arrived at Dolingers. She eased Kaia down on a chair covered by the porch awning and looked her over.

"You still with me?" Reza asked, both hands on Kaia's shoulders, kneeling to get a good look at her condition.

"Y-yeah," Kaia said, but her voice was thin and worrying.

They were soaked through, and Reza was concerned for the girl. If they were forced to keep moving, on foot and exposed to the weather, Kaia might start struggling to keep her strength in the chill rain. But Reza knew what she had come for was worth the risk—if he would listen to her.

"I'll be right back," Reza said. Kaia attempted a weak nod.

She opened the inn door and entered, drenched and miserable looking, enough of a sight to cause the inn's patrons to stare for a moment longer than was comfortable. Reza didn't care at that point.

Seldrin was moving toward her, seeing the distress in her features. Noticing the amount of attention on them, he backed her out the door and closed it behind him.

"What's wrong?" he asked. He could see it was more than just the rain that had the saren distressed. Before Reza could speak, Seldrin noticed Kaia slumped over in her chair, and he rushed to check on her.

"Were you two attacked?" he asked. Kaia was conscious, though shivering and sickly pale.

"Not exactly," Reza confessed. "The church followed us. They're on a manhunt."

"Did they follow you here?" Seldrin asked, moving to heft Kaia up from her wet seat.

Reza went to help. "I don't think so. Hard to track in this rain. Think we made it out of there clean."

"She needs to get dried off and into a bed, now," Seldrin ordered. He opened the inn door, and everyone eyed them once more.

"Room," he called out to the innkeeper. The man behind the counter led them out of the commons and down a hall to the back rooms. Opening the door for them, he ushered the three into a small bedroom that smelled of cedar. Seldrin began to remove Kaia's outer clothes as Reza asked the innkeeper for additional blankets and hot broth.

"What happened to her?" Seldrin asked as he threw back the sheets of the bed and gently placed

Kaia down on top.

"She performed a healing. She's just drained, but we had to pack up and flee right after that. Bad timing," Reza explained as she lit a candle.

Seldrin folded the sheets and quilt over Kaia, tucking her in bed, then stood back to assess her condition. She was calm, as though she would fall asleep at any moment.

The innkeeper arrived with hot broth and two extra quilts, handing both off to Reza and Seldrin.

As Reza sat at Kaia's bedside, helping her to sit up to take a sip of the steamy drink, Seldrin unfolded the blankets and placed them across her, then grabbed a towel to wring out her dripping hair.

"Mm, hot," she announced, still shivering.

Reza grabbed the pitcher of water in the room and poured a bit in the broth to cool it down, then tried again. Kaia sipped some and bobbed her head in approval. She took another few sips until her body began to warm up, helping her shivers to calm.

Reza took the drink from her while Seldrin helped her to lay back in bed, whispering for her to try and get some rest.

She was drifting asleep when Reza asked Seldrin in a hushed whisper, "Where's Jake and Neri?"

Seldrin shifted his attention from Kaia, now that she seemed to be doing better. "They're staying in another inn in town tonight. Told them that I'd be staying here and that I'd connect up with them on the morrow."

Reza briefly considered the implications of Seldrin's lodging plans. "You were planning on spending the night here?"

"Didn't know how long we'd chat for. Didn't want to cut our visit short just to avoid an annoying walk through town at an ungodly hour," he said, still watching Kaia's breathing.

Reza took a seat next to Kaia, gently wringing out her soaked hair and patting her face dry. Seldrin began pacing the small, dusty room.

"We would have stayed at the barracks as usual. Alumin always sets up visiting military with board and meals, but..." He trailed off. "Not this time. Something feels off about this town." Seldrin paused. "The church is hunting you?"

Reza watched as Kaia slept, her body no longer shivering, her breathing much more at peace now that she was warm and resting. "Yes. I recognized the White Cloak at the capitol building. He was the church worker that tracked me down and offered the audience with Prophet Yunus. Might have tracked us after we left the judicial district."

"But why?" Seldrin asked.

"Not sure of the exact reason. Maybe they've gotten word of Rosewood and suspect I was involved. I mean, they do know my history of involving myself with matters like these."

After that thought lingered for a moment, she added, "That they're hunting us down isn't the reason I came to you, though."

"There's more?" Seldrin asked in a flat tone.

"Yeah. A lot more. The church of Elendium hasn't worshiped the *actual* Elendium for some time. They've been systematically taken over by the cult of Umbraz. All high-ranking clergy have been working toward some breakthrough manifestation of this secret god for years now. Their goals are mass genocide of not just their own congregation, but all souls they can get their hands on."

Reza watched Seldrin, trying to gauge if he was following what she was saying. He was listening intently, though made no show of whether he believed her story.

She proceeded. "On top of that, they've been slowly gaining power in the government. State officials are stepping aside for them. They've effectively taken over the governing class within Alumin this year, and they've attempted the same for at least the Black Crowns and the Rediron kingdoms."

"Hold on. You're saying the church of Elendium is, in reality, some sort of death cult? And that they're taking control of the Crowned Kingdoms behind the scenes?"

Reza nodded.

Seldrin scratched his chin and frowned. "I'm going to be honest with you, Reza, that's a lot to take. If I hadn't seen the way your case has been handled, I'd call bullshit without hesitation. This is a lot to think over."

"You don't believe me?"

"Not at face value, no," he admitted. "There's enough here that's piqued my interest, though."

She hid her feelings well, but truthfully, she was crestfallen. She had her worries confirmed with Fin's findings, but even before that, she had thought long and hard on the strange vision she had received back in Rosewood. She knew the heart of this enemy. They were obsessed with bringing Umbraz into their realm. She wasn't quite sure how they planned to go about it, but having Seldrin on her side, and potentially the Silver Crowns along with him, would go a long way in gathering the strength to oppose the cult.

He threw up a hand, exasperated. "Why did you come to me? What do you want me to do about all this?"

Reza sighed. "Fin and I are looking into a group known as the Kingsmen—"

"The Kingsmen?" he interrupted.

"You've heard of them?"

"They're a terrorist group. Very elusive, I've heard. Been a thorn in the Black Steel Crown's kingdom and Alumin for some time, ever since the

Black Steel king was ousted."

Reza was growing tired of Seldrin's contempt. She did not guard her words. "We're seeking an audience with the Lost King now."

A knock came at the door. The innkeeper called to them from the other side. "Sir, Miss—you've got a fellow asking for you in the lobby. Seems urgent."

Reza opened the door and stepped out of the room, asking the man quietly, "Did he give you his name?"

"No, miss," he answered with a heavy local drawl. "He's a tan fellow. Strapped with more than a few knives."

Reza relaxed, not realizing that she had been so tense just a moment earlier. "Can you send him back here?"

"Yes, Miss," he readily agreed, and returned to the main room.

"Fin's here," Reza announced to Seldrin as she stepped back into the bedroom. It was apparent the news was not comforting to the general.

"I know an outlaw when I see one," he grumbled. "What's he got to do with all of this?"

She wanted to contest the remark, but she decided not to get into it with Seldrin just then. After all, Fin was an outlaw in multiple territories. She'd be hard-pressed to convince the man otherwise.

"He's our connection with the Kingsmen," she said.

"Of course he is," Seldrin replied incredulously. "That group—they're just a bunch of disruptors, Reza. They're a band of terrorists. I don't know what's going on with Alumin, but I can assure you the Kingsmen aren't working toward an equitable solution to Alumin's recent problems." Seldrin sighed, his fingers pushing against his temple.

Reza didn't respond to his concerns, so Seldrin pressed forward with his point. "Don't fall in with this group. You and Kaia are good people, I can tell. This *Fin* and the Kingsmen are nothing but trouble. Don't get caught up in it with them."

"A warm hello to you too, Mr. General," Fin remarked as he turned the corner and entered the room. Seldrin glared back.

"Reza, we need to leave town—now," Fin said, tugging on Reza's elbow.

"Kaia's resting," Reza replied, motioning to the soundly asleep saren.

Fin frowned. "I've secured passage in a covered wagon. We can make a bed for her and Nomad in the back."

"Kaia shouldn't be traveling anywhere in her state," Seldrin cut in.

Reza shook her head. "She's going to be in much worse condition if the church gets a hold of her."

"The question is, how come you care what becomes of either of these two gals?" Fin interjected, stepping between Reza and Seldrin. "What? You think you've got a chance at getting into their pants? Forget it, mate. That one's too young for you," he said, pointing to Kaia, "and this one has a lover already."

"Fin!" Reza scolded, warning her friend that he was dangerously close to being slapped.

Seldrin didn't answer Fin's provocation, but the glare he was giving the roguish man was reply enough for the message to come across loud and clear. If Reza and Kaia were not present, Seldrin would have made sure Fin had closed his mouth.

"Reza. We need to go. Our window of opportunity is fast closing," Fin said.

Reza watched Seldrin a moment longer, taking note of how affected he was by Fin's snide attitude.

"Where's your wagon?" Reza asked.

"It's out front. Nomad is already loaded in the back. I can help get Kaia in there. You bring the blankets; I'll pay the innkeeper for them and carry Kaia out."

"You're really going to transport her in that condition?" Seldrin asked Reza, pointing to Kaia, who slumbered peacefully in bed.

"Seldrin, we have no choice," she said, fatigue in her voice. "Do you honestly think it would be better for us to get snatched up by church thugs and prosecuted in their synagogue? A fever is a better fate than lingering in some church dungeon because we saw what we shouldn't have in Rosewood."

Seldrin gave Reza a hard, judging look. It was clear Reza was set on the plan—*Fin's* plan. He turned to Fin. "I'll carry Kaia, *you* pay the innkeeper."

Fin didn't argue the point. The three gathered their things and Kaia and rushed out of the room. Seldrin carried Kaia, still asleep, wrapped up in a bundle of blankets and sheets.

Fewer patrons were in the front room now. Those that remained made way for the group as they hauled Kaia and their things outside. Hunching over the girl to protect her from the rain, Seldrin rushed after the others and handed her up to Reza and Fin, who took her into the shelter of the waxed fabric cover over the wagon.

"Finish loading, but don't leave without me," he called above the drone of the downpour.

Rushing back inside and calling once again to the innkeeper, who had given up all hopes of tending to his other duties, Seldrin asked for paper and quill. He quickly scrawled a few lines and blew on the parchment before folding it once, pouring wax from a nearby candle on the seam. He stamped it sealed with his signet ring.

Handing it to the innkeeper, he commanded in a hushed whisper, "Two soldiers from Silver Crowns will come looking for me tomorrow; Jake and Neri.

Deliver this to them—and only them."

The innkeeper agreed. Without another word, Seldrin rushed out to the wagon that was ready to depart, loaded up with Reza, Kaia, Fin, and Nomad in the back with two fellows in dark rain gear up at the front, ready to drive the two-horse team onward as soon as he jumped aboard.

He held onto the side of the covered frame, watching the inn as they slowly retreated down the city road into the rainy night. He half expected to see White Cloaks and the city guard show up just before they turned the bend. Instead, the streets were dark and empty, rain obscuring anything further than a city block.

Ducking his head under the cover, he took stock of the ragged crew of misfits. He did not hide his displeasure at whom Reza traveled with.

Fin looked equally disgusted with the general's presence and leaned in to whisper something in Reza's ear.

"I'm haltia, rogue. Whatever you have to say to Reza, I'm going to hear it whether you wish me to or not. Speak your piece openly when I'm around."

Fin didn't hesitate to ask, "Why are you here, soldier boy?"

Seldrin had no answer for him. In fact, it was a question he'd asked himself the moment he had set foot in the wagon.

CHAPTER 18 - SOUNDS OF BATTLE

The rain had persisted throughout the night, and the riders only stopped a few times for the horses' sakes. With the day now dawned and the heavy cloud cover finally showing signs of breaking, the riders pulled to the side of the highway along a flat bank near an outcropping of trees to rest and water the horses properly. The rest of the crew got out to stretch and throw open the back wagon flap to allow fresh air and light in for a proper assessment of Nomad and Kaia's condition.

Upon sunlight gracing her face, Kaia winced and rolled over. Her color looked much better. Reza gently patted her back, then looked to Nomad to see how he fared.

"How's the hip?" she asked. Though Nomad had been up for the last hour, he had been very quiet and reserved.

"The pain is bearable, now," he grumbled, his voice still ragged.

"Think you can walk on it?" Reza asked. By the end of the day, they would arrive at their destination. Nomad would need to relocate eventually.

"I will give it a try," he replied. Now was a good time to test how thorough Kaia's healing had been.

Reza helped him up from his blankets in the corner. He slowly made his way off the back of the covered wagon as Seldrin held the flap open for them. Reza helped Nomad down off the back gate.

Nomad let go of Reza's shoulder and took a few steps into the meadow, tenderly testing his gait. Gaining a bit of confidence as his hip held his weight, he made his way to a tree and gingerly took a seat on a raised root. He allowed himself a small smile as he looked back to Reza, who had been watching him.

She returned his smile and glanced back to Seldrin.

The haltia had also been quiet, secluded with his thoughts throughout the night, and he was no different now. He had not been watching Nomad's mobility test, though. She saw that he was focused on someone else in the wagon, and his expression was not a kindly one.

Reza realized that he was eyeing Fin in the corner of the dim wagon. Fin seemed to be asleep resting his eyes, but upon further inspection, she got the feeling something seemed off about her friend.

"He's septic, I believe," Seldrin said to Reza in a low voice. "I've been keeping an eye on him all night. He's favoring his side—looks like there's some seepage through his undercoat. I can smell something putrid from him, and I don't think it's just his body odor."

Reza could see the dark patch under his cloak now that Seldrin pointed it out.

"Gut wounds are vicious creditors," said Seldrin. "Last night's exertion likely cost him greatly. Today's going to be hell for him."

She jumped up in the wagon to get a closer look at Fin and rested a hand on his shoulder, nudging him slightly.

"Fin?" she called.

He didn't answer. His color was a deep yellow. A cold sweat formed on her brow. It had been so dark through the night that she had figured he had just been resting. But his health had been deteriorating dramatically.

She looked to Kaia again. There was no way she was going to ask Kaia for another healing so soon, even with her looking much better from the previous night, but Fin needed a saren's touch immediately.

She refused to look at Seldrin or tell him what she was about to do. She knew he'd attempt to talk her out of it or even try to stop her. She gave a silent prayer and pressed a hand upon Fin's chest.

Breathing deeply, she fell into his spirit's aether flow, centering in on his wound and attempting to assess the extent of the damage.

She could instantly feel malignancy in Fin's body, a putrid patch of harm festering in his side. She needed to neutralize the infection and seal the gut wall.

He roused, and though she was deep in a meditative state, she sensed he was groaning, moving out of protest—though conscious or not, she couldn't tell. Either way, it was making her healing much more difficult.

She forced a surge of life essence into his malaise, dispersing much of the infection, emulsifying bacteria responsible for Fin's lethargy.

The wave of energy had cost her greatly, but she sent another surge to ensure the area was cleansed.

She trembled, groaning with the effort the healing was exacting. Again, she could feel resistance from Fin. Distantly she could hear him telling her to *stop*. He was awake and aware that she was spending her life force on reviving him.

She couldn't stop now, not with the laceration so deep in his side. It would simply become reinfected if she didn't close it up now.

She pressed on, spending the rest of her energy to fuse his inner and outer tissues back together.

Reza fell into blackness, her consciousness draining into a quiet void.

"Shadowcliff Castle ain't but a few miles more ride down the road. Ready your group for inspections. The Lost King is thorough with new visitors," the lead rider called back to Fin from his seat up front.

Fin looked at Reza, leaning against Nomad. Nomad had watched over her the bulk of the day as they rode, cushioning her from the jostle of the bumpy ride they had endured. Kaia sat pensively at Reza's side, watching over her older counterpart.

The young saren had suggested another healing, but Fin had denied her. Perhaps it was the wrong move, but he had had enough of the healings wiping the two girls out. It would only be a game of chasing diminishing returns. He had seen Reza at death's door too many times to allow her to go down that path without dire need.

"Nomad, how is she faring?" Fin asked softly.

"Same." His voice was low with concern.

Fin's glower did not fade as he eyed Seldrin on the other side of the cart. Seldrin embodied all the unyielding elements of the law Fin had been on the opposing side of since his youth. The man's movements, words, looks…everything about him spoke of a long history of upright service in law enforcement. Such men rarely had room for understanding others' unique circumstances in their gauntleted judgments. Most came equipped with an unhealthy and overbearing certainty about what was right and what was wrong. Fin hated pious bastards like Seldrin, and he sorely regretted not taking a stand against Reza when she had rushed to recruit him.

Not only did he not like the man in general, but he had no idea about his motives for joining

them. The best he could figure was that the haltia
had a thing for Reza. Perhaps Seldrin wished to
uncover the resistance group's hideout and report it
to the authorities. That could very possibly be the
motivation behind his actions, but Fin doubted even
one so devout to law and his country would place
himself so far behind enemy lines, alone. It would
be too foolhardy of a man likely well-versed in risk
assessment and tactics.

If it wasn't either of those, then Fin was
genuinely at a loss for why the haltia was there. He
didn't like unknown motives.

"What's the king's son's name again?" Fin asked
the rider not engaged with the reins.

"Warchief Waldock," the man answered.

Fin committed the surname to memory. For the
most part, everyone had just referred to the king as
the Lost King, but Fin had learned that the Lost King's
family had a rich history. The queen had taken back
her maiden name when she cast her husband out of
power years ago.

He had heard briefly about the Mad Queen
during his stay in Rediron country. He now knew that
she was known as Queen Sabat to her countrymen.
She had married into royalty with King Waldock and
slowly turned the kingdom against the king's own
subjects by planting degrading rumors. The takeover
had been the talk of the kingdoms when she struck
out against them, and she had taken the throne and

crown with the support of the corrupted militia and the approval of the people.

Those loyal to the king withdrew with him to a distant region of the realm, and there they had established and secured a territory that the queen struggled to crack, even after years of campaigns.

That was how he had understood it, at least. He had done his best to extrapolate the truth from the biases and outlandish claims of the Lost King's supporters.

"His lord's given name is Johnathan, but you'd not want to open with that upon introduction, unless you don't mind hanging from a high tree," the lead rider added after a silence.

"Right," Fin agreed, idly rubbing a hand over his neck. He had been hung before…he didn't need to tempt the fates again. A cat only had so many lives, after all.

"Now, there's someone back there able to help unload the haul of foodstuffs when we arrive, right?" the rider asked Fin.

"Yeah. I'll be good for it," Fin replied as happily as he could muster, given the circumstances. "My friends have taken a turn for the worst, though. They're a bit under the weather."

"Nothin' contagious, I hope?"

"No, no," Fin assured him, then retreated to join the others in the back of the wagon.

PAULYODER

Fin let out a sigh, sitting back against the wagon's bed wall, and rested his eyes for a moment. The non-stop pace of the last few months was catching up with him. His mind wasn't as sharp as he needed it to be. To have forgotten a key player's name...he couldn't afford to let important data slip like that—names especially. It was the familiar use of a person's name that separated a stranger from an associate—the first step in developing useful relationships.

He opened his eyes only to see Seldrin staring at him. Just the sight of the man irked him.

Fin sat up. "I don't know why you're here, but if you're going to be with us, you're going to pull your weight. Once we arrive, I expect you to help us unload this wagon with the riders while I tend to Reza and the crew."

"I can do that," Seldrin answered.

"Good." Fin shifted to try and get comfortable in the rough wooden wagon bed.

He looked to Nomad and softened his tone considerably. "How are you doing, ol' chap?"

"I can walk on my own," Nomad replied. "I might not be able to run quite yet, but my hip feels worlds better than it did a day ago."

"That's something, at least." Fin looked over Reza again, who was resting soundly. He leaned close to Nomad and whispered, "We'll need to be on our

198

toes once we arrive at the Lost King's domain. I hear it takes a lot to earn the trust of the king and his son. But if we can, they would make powerful allies in the fight with the White Cloaks. As I understand it, the Lost King was the first target of the cult of Umbraz. We have a common enemy, which goes a long way in making a case for our cooperation."

Nomad nodded once more. "I may not be as mobile as you for a while, but I can stay with the girls. I will not let harm come upon them."

"Good man," Fin said, patting Nomad's shoulder approvingly.

"Oi," one of the riders called back in a hushed but urgent tone.

Fin poked his head out of the front flap.

"Something's not right up ahead," the rider whispered. He pulled up on the reins and slowed the horses to a halt.

"Sounds like a battle," Seldin commented. He joined Fin at the front of the wagon.

"Sure does," the rider agreed.

"Wait." Seldrin's ears perked up as he looked the way they had come. "Is this the only road?"

"There are a few trails in these parts. Why?" the rider asked.

"We need to get off the main road," Seldrin said. The authority of a commander came through in his tone and spurred the rider into action.

"James, head around the side path through the ruins," the wingman said to his fellow rider as he pointed out the path.

"How many?" Fin asked Seldrin, knowing the advantage the haltia had over his human counterparts.

"Four or five, maybe. On horseback, moving fast." Seldrin returned to the interior of the wagon to strap on his sword belt and string his bow.

He clambered up to sit on the end of the rider's deck and stood to get a better view behind them. Fin made his way to the back of the wagon, hanging off the frame to cover their rear. They were posted defensibly. Though Fin hadn't wished the haltia's company up until now, the general had the poise and demeanor of someone who knew how to hold his own in combat.

"Dust along the road—not ours," Seldrin called. "They're following us and moving in fast."

"Wait for us to identify them," the rider ordered Seldrin, who now had an arrow nocked. "If you fire upon a Kingsmen detachment, you'll sign our death warrant."

Seldrin nodded. The wagon rolled out into an open field. Rubble and remains of battlements were scattered across the once-developed land at the base of the old castle, which now came into view once they were out of tree cover.

"Make for the gate—there!" the wingman yelled to the rider, and pointed him to an old, overgrown path through a town long succumbed to the wild, now more a harbor for woodland creatures than man.

The four riders breached the tree line at last. Black-oiled armor lent the flash force an ominous aura. Despite being fully armored, they rode at such a pace that they were quickly catching up with the weaving wagon. Black cloaks with the Mad Queen's emblem tapered behind them and the sharp point of a knight's longsword led them forward. Seldrin called them out for the wingman.

"Not ours," he said, sitting back down as the wagon threatened to shiver apart from passing over the rough terrain. "Those are Black Guards—Mad Queen's men. They'll kill us if they catch up to us."

"Fin. Make ready to defend our rear," Seldrin called out.

Fin, holding to the side of the wagon with one hand and gripping a throwing dagger in the other, needed no prompt to be on guard. He was already waiting to see the whites of the lead rider's eyes. He itched to unleash hell upon the Black Steel soldiers.

CHAPTER 19 - SKIRMISH AT THE RUINS

The wagon suddenly jostled as a wheel cracked into an outcropping of rubble, shaking everyone on the vehicle.

Reza had been rousing before the crash, but now she and Kaia were fully awake. Nomad filled them in on the situation as Fin and the others up front struggled to hang on to their seats.

Turning toward the castle, the rider could see a melee up ahead by the battlements at the old gate. Figuring that was their best chance at receiving backup, and also guessing they'd all be dead if they didn't get support soon, he snapped the reins frantically, spurring the two horses forward at break-neck speeds toward the main battlefront as the queen's knights weaved closer and closer to the rear of the wagon.

Seldrin took aim but hesitated. Opening fire on another kingdom's troops was an act of war, but the speed and approach showed that the gang of knights meant to ravage them—not to stop and ask questions.

He was in an unwinnable situation, but if he had to make a choice between bad and worse, he'd pick the path that might see him live another day. He loosed an arrow at the nearest knight. The point deflected harmlessly off the slanted black helm.

A throwing dagger spun toward the same rider and clanged off the knight's gorget. The knights charged on, showing no acknowledgment of the projectiles. The lead knight was upon the back of the wagon within moments. Fin drew his sapphire-pommeled longsword, readying to ward off the coming assault.

The wagon jolted up in the air suddenly, its wheel bursting from the impact of another pile of stone. Fin held on to the frame, somehow managing to not impale himself, and kept a grip on his sword as he was thrown up onto the canvas wagon roof.

The knights charged past and moved to circle back around the busted wagon that had come to an unexpected stop.

Fin and Seldrin were none the worse for wear. Fin had landed atop the forgiving stretched canvas. Seldrin had tucked and rolled into the grass to the roadside. The horses were raging, attempting to untangle themselves from the mess of reins and towing struts, which were causing trouble for the Kingsmen riders. One attempted to pull the other out of harm's way of the horse's flailing limbs.

"Up on your feet!" Seldrin called to the

Kingsmen. The knights had circled and were now coming in on them for a strafing pass.

The driver dropped his unconscious companion and rolled out of reach of the first knight's sword point, but the second knight was close behind, casually swinging his longsword low. He lopped off the arm of the driver running back to the wagon for safety.

The other two knights came to a halt at the unconscious driver, dismounted, and ran the man through, then stepped over his dead body to approach the wagon while the two mounted riders rushed on toward Seldrin's position.

Seldrin looped his cloak around his arm and drew his saber in his other, waiting to make his move as the two knights ran down upon him.

The first charged hard and fast, swinging in a long arc rather than thrusting, seeing the fabric in the man's hand for what it was.

Seldrin rolled out of the way, knowing the sword would have easily sliced through his cloak if he had attempted to block the powerful cut with it. The next knight charged sword tip first, thinking to catch the haltia off guard as he came out of his tumble. Seldrin was quick on the recovery though. He batted at the thrusting sword with his cloak, binding around it and ripping it down out of the knight's grip as he rode past.

The knight had committed too heavily to the

fighting move, which knocked him off-balance. He fell sideways on his saddle before toppling off a few yards past Seldrin.

Seldrin rushed toward the downed man, attempting to strike while the knight was dazed, but the other knight was quick to his comrade's aid and leaped off his horse to engage Seldrin.

There was the clang of steel as the knight pressed Seldrin hard, backing him away from his comrade, who was now up. Recovering his dropped sword, the knight circled around to flank the haltia.

Seldrin knew he had lost his window. The fight was now going to be much more arduous with two foes than one. The two-handed longswords were more mobile than his single-handed saber. Perhaps if the knights were not in full plate mail the fight would have been a bit fairer, but his typical style of hand and shin targeting would only be putting himself in vulnerable positions. He would need to resort to other tactics if he wished to even the field.

He sidestepped a sword swipe and positioned himself away from the flanking knight, keeping the two working their footwork rather than focusing their attention on attacks.

He rolled, dodging another thrust of the knight's sword, scooping up some gravel as he went.

He was up, narrowly sidestepping a quick swipe from the knight as he pressed forward to close the gap once again. Seldrin slapped the knight's blade wide, then flung the handful of dirt and stones directly at his helm before he had a chance to riposte.

Seldrin stepped back as the knight swung blindly for a moment. The other knight saw the move and rushed in, but it was too late. Seldrin stepped in past the knight's guard, gripping the man by the sword wrist, and planted a leg behind him. In one fluid motion, he tripped him, flinging him backward and disarming him at the same time.

Seldrin had moved in a blur. As the other knight rushed up to his ally, the red crimson of the Black Guard's arterial blood along the gorget seam was a chilling sign that he would not be returning to the fight.

The first battle yell sounded, the knight at once enraged that an unarmored foe had bested one of his own but also fearful, knowing it was now a one-on-one fight.

The yell had emboldened the knight, and he pressed hard into Seldrin's defenses. A few close calls caused the haltia to stumble back into the rubble of an old, overgrown building.

Rolling over the low wall and in under the rotted-out rafters, he wrapped his cloak around his arm once more and batted at the knight's sword as it chopped in at him.

He'd been lucky with the throat thrust at the other knight. The seams between this knight's armor were well-fitted and tight. He knew he needed to consider other options. He did not wish to roll the dice once more.

Rolling back over a table, he rushed into the next room as the knight crashed through the moldy wood.

The knight rushed into the dark room and stopped in his tracks as he looked for signs of his foe. Seeing no exit, he took a step in to peer around a rotting beam in the center of the room.

His vision went black as Seldrin threw his cloak over his helmet. Seldrin was behind him, out of reach of his swing, and kicked him from behind, sending the knight barreling through the beam in the center of the room.

Seldrin rushed over the threshold as the roof crumpled in. The creaky rafters came down in a cloud of dust, sealing the knight in the bosom of the old house.

He waited a moment to see if the knight stirred —he couldn't see anything but a billowing dust cloud. He rushed back to the wagon, hoping that Fin was as capable with his daggers as he was with his prejudices.

A bolt thudded into the ground at his feet, slowing his stride. He glanced around for the shooter. It didn't take him long.

Upon a grassy knoll at the border of the ruins, the crossbowman called out to him; there was a group of volley men ready with three more loaded crossbows led by a large rough-looking knight. The knight called out now that they had Seldrin's attention.

"Hold your position!" the man shouted. "Identify yourself."

Seldrin looked to where he had left his companions. More of the same troops were already upon the crashed wagon. He was too late to help if the hailing force belonged to the enemy.

"Seldrin of the Silver Crowns. I'm with that supplies' caravan headed for the Lost King's domain."

The man made a sign for the crossbowmen to lower their weapons. "Then you're with us. Go see to your people."

Seldrin needed no further prompting. Rushing to the covered wagon, he arrived just as Nomad assisted a very banged-up and bruised Reza and Kaia out of the back of the wagon bed.

The foot soldiers overseeing the scene looked at Seldrin, on relaxed guard.

"Reza, Kaia, are you both alright?" he asked.

"That's the last time we take a fucking wagon instead of a coach," Reza grumbled, clutching a goose egg on her forehead.

Seldrin cracked a smile. Nomad wasn't smiling when he ordered Seldrin to go make sure Fin was alright.

Seldrin rushed to the other side of the wagon,

where he found more footmen huddled around the driver's area, hauling a few bodies off the field.

He approached the huddle of soldiers just as Fin rose with the injured driver, a tourniquet clamping off the flow of blood from his gory nub.

Handing the man over to a foot soldier, Fin looked down at the knight under his heel and shoved him over on his back.

"The other one's dead, but this one should still be breathing. Make sure you restrain him before he comes around," Fin said.

Turning his attention to Seldrin now that the injured and dead were handed over to the Kingsmen troops, he asked, "You leave either of yours alive?"

"They're dead," Seldrin said, still catching his breath.

"Of course they are." Fin bumped Seldrin's shoulder as he stormed past him to help Nomad with the two dazed women. "Make yourself useful and gather our things," Fin called out to Seldrin as he looped Kaia's arm around his shoulder.

Seldrin slammed his sword into his scabbard, then snatched up his bow and headed to the back of the wagon to gather the group's things.

"As annoying as he is degenerate," Seldrin grumbled. Looking to the four soldiers still at the scene, he pointed to the wagon and called, "Foodstuffs are in the wagon. Courtesy of the Kingsmen in

Alumin."

Running to catch up to Reza and the rest of the group, he arrived just as they approached the man in command flanked by four crossbowmen who had been waiting for them.

"That was an impressive display," the man said in a low baritone. "The queen's Black Guard are no pushovers. I should know. I trained them."

The juxtaposed statement gave Fin and Seldrin cause for pause, wondering who it was that addressed and assessed them.

"Come. The battle's over—for now at least," the man ordered with the wave of a gauntleted hand. He took his helmet off to let down a shock of unruly crow-black hair, a great scar along one side of his face. "I wish to know who slays Black Guard so casually."

CHAPTER 20 - EXHAUSTED AND BATTERED

"Do you have any injured among your group?" the scarred man asked as they made their way back to the towering castle, passing through the partially broken gates and outer wall.

"Some are still recovering from previous hardships," Fin answered for Reza, seeing that she and Kaia were completely spent. Nomad wasn't faring so well either. Fin could see that he was squinting with pain from walking so far on his freshly healed hip.

"Who are you lot? I gather you accompanied a supply run of our men in Alumin, but I've no knowledge of Silver Crowns joining our cause, and I've never seen you, Southerner," the man asked of Fin.

"Our story...is complicated," Fin admitted. He paused as the man received reports from another band that rode up to connect with the leader before heading off into a covered stable in the shadows of the old castle.

"Close the gates; that should be everyone," the man boomed back down the line. "Stand watch. Those bastards retreated, but they could turn face and come back for a rallying strike."

"Do you wish to retire before we continue our conversation?" the leader asked directly to Fin, having no time for idle talk with the newcomers.

"That would be appreciated," Fin answered.

"Josiah!"

A soldier with face tattoos ran up silently from behind them.

Between orders to other groups of soldiers, the war leader addressed Josiah. "See this lot to an empty room in the guest wing. Watch them. I'll come visit later this evening once things settle down in the war room."

"Aye, chief," the man said, looking Fin in the eyes. He motioned for the group to follow him. They branched off from the main warband and headed to a smaller wing of the castle to the side of the main entrance.

The old wing of the castle seemed rarely used, its furnishings moldering and dilapidated, upholstery faded and ragged. Josiah took a candle from the center table and led the group back through the dark halls. A cool draft sent shivers through Kaia as they made their way to the first open room.

Thankfully, it was one of the largest rooms in the wing, and there was plenty of sitting and cot space for the group to stretch out in.

Deep soot marks above the hearth pit and worn timber floorboards indicated that the place had been well lived in in times past, but it was clear that the room had not been in use of late. Hanging from the walls were tapestries, emblemed shields, sets of cross swords, but all were rotting or rusted. Cobwebs and dust clung to most of the furnishings.

Fin eased Kaia down on a couch while Nomad put Reza down on a cot and took the one next to her for himself. Seldrin went to place their gear on the table in the study section of the room while Fin grabbed a blanket from amongst their things to cover Kaia up.

"Uhh," Reza moaned, clutching at her head. Her shiner had turned a dark, blueish purple.

"A headache?" Nomad asked, sitting up with some effort.

She only moaned.

"Fin, my pack." Nomad snapped his fingers and pointed to his things. Fin brought it over. Seldrin came over to see for himself what ailed the saren.

"I could perform a healing if—" Kaia began.

"Damn it, Kaia. Get some rest, girl," Fin cut her off.

Nomad shuffled through his side pouches and took out a metal canister packed full of powders and herbs. Taking a few pinches of green and yellow powder, he pointed to the candle. "Bring me the light."

Seldrin approached Josiah and asked the soldier to fetch water for them. The man didn't seem happy about leaving the group alone in the guest wing but relented as Reza's color began to fade rapidly. He ran off in search of water.

"Damn," Reza moaned, opening her eyes to reveal completely dilated pupils. "I can't see."

She was slurring. Kaia got up and approached her.

"I can help," she insisted, but Fin held an arm out to keep her from touching Reza.

"The last thing we need is both of you on the floor out cold," Fin snipped.

Nomad had lit a bit of spice in the flame and wafted the sparkling dust toward Reza. The room filled with a foreign, aromatic scent, sharpening the senses of everyone in the huddle.

Reza roused slightly at the smell, and after a few more inhales of the aroma, Josiah rushed back into the room with a silver pitcher and cup. He handed them both over to Seldrin.

"You still can't see, Reza?" Nomad asked.

"I…" she started but trailed off, her eyes slowly closing independent of one another.

Nomad elevated her legs slightly, placing them on his lap. "Keep her awake. Keep her talking," he ordered Fin.

"Hey, ol' girl, you need to stay with us, okay?" Fin said loudly, kneeling, brushing her hair back from her eyes. "I'm no saren but I'm going to say, you shouldn't be attempting a healing again for a good while. Fair enough?" Fin tried to keep her attention glued on him, but she was struggling with keeping her eyes open.

"Breathe, Reza," Fin said, placing a hand lightly on her stomach. "Take some deep breaths from down in your core."

To everyone's relief, Fin's words seemed to make it through to her, and her chest did rise as she started to take in unsteady breaths, albeit slowly at first.

Color began to trickle through her features. Her pupils slowly reduced.

"Good job." Fin smiled, brushing her hair to the side. "Looking better. Nomad. Another pinch of that stimulant powder, please."

Nomad handed him the can and candle. Fin burned the spice once more. This time, the effect seemed to rouse Reza more effectively.

Looking around, her eyes mostly back to normal and her color clearly back, she asked, "I...can see again. What just happened to me?"

No one immediately answered. She cupped her hands over her face, trembling.

"Perhaps you overdid it with your healing this morning?" Fin suggested.

"Or maybe that bump on your head was more serious than you thought it was," Seldrin said. "Or maybe it was a combination of the two."

She looked to Nomad, wanting his opinion on the worrying episode more so than anyone else. Nomad cleared his voice and offered, "Your body is telling you to slow down, Reza Malay. If you don't, it will force you to."

The others nodded their agreement.

Fin stood up, running his hands through his hair, pacing the room. His thoughts were everywhere. Taking his own advice, he took some slow, deliberate breaths to calm his nerves.

The whole crew was worn ragged. Nomad, Kaia, and Reza had it the worst, but Fin still felt slightly sick from his gut wound. Though it was healed, he couldn't help but feel ghost pains from his side, as if his flesh was telling him that it remembered the trauma he had put it through.

He had been going non-stop since arriving in the Crowned Kingdoms. He worried he would soon be sharing the sickbed with Reza if he didn't wind down at some point.

A soldier walked into the tense room. "Josiah, everything all right here?"

"Yeah, just one of them had a bit of an episode," Josiah whispered back.

The soldier gave the group a brief moment out

of respect but soon asked the question he had been sent to deliver. "Who speaks for your group?"

Fin looked around a moment and realized that neither Reza nor Nomad would be in a state to answer for the group.

Raising his hand, he offered, "I do."

"The warchief wishes to speak with you," the soldier ordered, waving Fin over.

Walking over to Seldrin, Fin whispered to the haltia, "You watch over them, you hear?"

Seldrin nodded, then Fin was off, stepping lively after the soldier who was already on his way out of the room.

Fin clenched his jaw and shored up his step. He couldn't afford to be on shaky footing now, not of limb or of mind. Maybe he did need a break—maybe they all did—but it was not in the cards. He needed to find the strength to push forward. If he broke, he broke; but until then, he would plunge head-first into their mission.

He matched the soldier's gait, resolve now carrying him forward, replacing the weight of doubt.

CHAPTER 21 - UPON THE WATCHTOWER

The castle was old, ancient even, but Fin could see some sections that the Lost King had set to refurbish and make usable again. The watchtower was one of those improvements.

New timbers and fresh masonry lined and filled in patches of the old structure. It was a wide tower, and easy to scale the spiral steps up to the top.

The sight of the countryside from that vantage point momentarily took Fin's full attention when he stepped foot onto the covered platform. A fresh forest breeze livened his senses.

"Now that's a sight," Fin remarked, entranced by the vivid contrast between the blue sky, white clouds, and glistening rolling hills of evergreens that had just been given a wash from the recent rainstorm.

"It's not the view I called you here for," the same scarred man from the battlefield said in a deep voice, still in his bloodied plate mail, save for his helmet.

Fin took note of the man standing before him, hand on the rail, overlooking the battlefront that had seen bloodshed earlier that day. He had been led to believe this was Johnathan Waldock, the Lost

King's warchief and son, though the man had yet to introduce himself.

"You the leader of that eclectic attachment accompanying my supply runners caravan?" the gruff man asked.

"Yes sir."

"You are to address me as warchief, lord, or Prince Waldock, whichever you prefer, but *sir*, I am not."

"Understood, my lord."

"You seem to be comprised of more than just hired hands. What are you?"

Fin considered the question a moment. The subject was fluid and complicated. He gave his best shot at summarizing it. He got the feeling very few were allowed to keep this man waiting for long.

"We each hail from different places and social strata. Until recently, I was enlisted under the command of Sultan Metus of the Plainstate, as was Reza Malay, the saren. Nomad is a foreigner from far to the east, good with the sword, and has accompanied us for many years now. Kaia is a saren stationed at West Perch, and the haltia is General Seldrin of the Silver Crowns kingdom. Kaia and General Seldrin have only just started traveling with us."

"I see. Eclectic indeed," the warchief mused. "And what business do you have associating yourself with the Kingsmen chapter in Alumin?"

Fin folded his arms. "Reza, Nomad, and I embarked to the Crowned Kingdoms to investigate a worrying vision of Reza's High Priestess, Lanereth. A close associate of ours went missing in the Rediron kingdom, so we set out to find him and uncover truths concerning Lanereth's premonitions."

"Kaia and General Seldrin?" the warlord prompted.

"Reza connected with Kaia at West Perch when seeking guidance from her order in this region. Kaia agreed to accompany her pilgrimage. General Seldrin...he connected with Reza some weeks ago, as I understand it, in Silver Crowns. I believe he has taken to Reza's quest as well, though I was separated from Reza at the time. I can't rightly speak for his or Kaia's character or motivation. All I know is they have helped us thus far and have sworn to support our cause. They have taken great risks to do so, which should count for something."

"If true, your troop boasts of some impressive credentials," the warchief said, looking out over the forest. "And how did you establish a connection to our movement?"

"That was my doing. It was clear upon our arrival that there was unrest amongst the people of Alumin. I fell into talks with Kingsmen and saw that our issues concerning the White Cloaks were aligned. We're looking to facilitate collaborations between interested nations and organizations to help address the White Cloak dilemma."

"That's noble of you."

"The cult of Umbraz is causing a great deal of pain throughout the land," Fin reasoned.

"So, you want to ally us with the Sarens, Silver Crowns, and Southern Sands…"

"And the Rediron kingdom," Fin amended.

The scarred man turned to face Fin; his grizzled visage gave Fin some pause. "The bastard King Maxim would see my father wiped from the face of the land. We have no commonality there, Sir Fin."

Fin considered his next words carefully. "King Maxim is dead, by my hand, in fact."

Judging by the man's incredulous glare, Fin saw his words had evoked something within the warchief.

Good, Fin thought. With men as intense as Johnathan, Fin had seen that strong impressions were needed in order for them to pay any others heed.

It was information he gave up at great risk. Being known as a king killer was not something he wanted to be public knowledge unless there was good reason to claim that title. Given Johnathan's initial reactions and words regarding the mad king, he took a gambit to ensure the warchief's full attention. All chips were out on the table now—though the cards had yet to be flipped.

"A bold claim. I've not even had word of his

assassination yet," the warchief said, eyeing Fin hard, his hand lingering close to his sword hilt. "Forgive me if I take your claim with some salt for now until I tap my network to confirm the news."

"By all means."

Johnathan paced for a moment, considering the news. "If I haven't yet had word of this assassination, and what you say *is* true, that would place his death no more than two weeks ago. Any more time and news surely would have reached me."

"That is about the timeline of events. No more than a week and a few days have passed since I was in the king's throne room."

"This would tag you as an assassin, then. Is this your trade?"

"I used to be a hitman, yes. Though in recent years, under the employment of Sultan Metus, I was utilized as a special operative. I haven't done assassin work for many years."

"Why start again now?"

Fin's mood sullied as he thought back on the wicked king. "King Maxim was poisoning his own people. I saw it firsthand, and my friend suffered because of it. He needed to be stopped, and no one else looked to be in a position to stop him from initiating the next phase of his designs with the Umbraz cultist."

Johnathan eyed Fin cautiously, fully aware that standing in the same space as an assassin without the protection of guards was a dangerous predicament. "Why then, cutthroat Fin, would you claim that the Rediron kingdom would be willing to join our cause? If the king is dead, the lords will be in squabbles over who should wear the crown. The last thing on anyone's mind is unifying in an alliance to help root out cult factions in other lands."

"I believe the kingdom's marshal rose to the occasion. I had talks with Marshal Reid in private. He's a good man and a sensible one. He has the support of the people. Last I saw, he made a move to take the crown, and no lord opposed him—likely because they knew they didn't have the support. The Rediron kingdom seems more unified now than ever, especially against White Cloaks."

Johnathan thought on Fin's words for some time, so long that Fin was beginning to worry that the warchief wasn't buying his story.

At length, he replied. "You've piqued my interest. I'll organize a meeting with King Waldock for you to go over the details of this proposed allyship."

Fin was relieved. He knew plenty of other commanders that would have thrown him in the dungeon solely for being an assassin. Johnathan seemed to Fin to be strict, but a man of thought and reason.

"For now, return to your people. Josiah will see to your needs in the meantime. Considering your profession, I'm going to have to ask you to stay within the guest wing. There is an attached garden in the back. Feel free to stretch your legs there, but I will have a few men keep posted to watch your crew. I hope you understand our precautions for now."

"Not a problem," Fin agreed. "Reza, Kaia, and Nomad have been pushing their bodies to the breaking point up until now. Some rest will do them good."

Johnathan nodded and dismissed him.

On his way back to the guest wing, Fin wondered if he had overstated his connections and their willingness to seek partnership with the Lost King's forces. Every single partnership he offered was a tentative one. He only hoped that his optimism about each state and organization had the foresight to see the threat the White Cloaks posed to their way of life.

CHAPTER 22 - CONVERSATIONS IN THE GARDEN

That night and the following day had been a time of recovery for Reza and the crew. Reza had slept through the rest of that evening into the next afternoon. Most accepted the downtime for what it was—a blessed reprieve from their hardships on the road. Nomad and Kaia both enjoyed naps throughout the day, gathering what strength they could in the cool, dim gallery room of the guest wing. Fin and Seldrin, however, were still on edge and found it difficult to slow down, waiting for word from the lords of the castle.

By late evening that day, Fin had spent time reorganizing their packs, and Seldrin had fully polished and cleaned his equipment and armament to an obsessive degree.

As the sun set, they both found their way out into the overgrown gardens, it being the only other space that they were allowed to roam apart from the guest wing.

Seldrin cleared his throat as he came across

Fin in the gardens' sitting area. Fin sat on a viny stone bench, wild roses in the area offering a thick floral aroma. He was choosing not to acknowledge the haltia.

"Fin, we need to clear the air between us if we are to be working together," Seldrin said, hands behind his back, overlooking the same vista.

The Black Steel countryside was similar to Rediron in a few notable ways. The evergreens were plentiful. Rich green grass covered the land save for the mountains that sprawled across the region like veins of the kingdom. Unlike Rediron, though, Black Steel country was higher in elevation. The air was crisper, and the mountains wore white caps of snow all along the range to the southwest. Fin appreciated the dramatic change of environment from the Southern Sands, where he had spent most of his life.

"Fin…" Seldrin said, his patience wearing thin.

"I'll ask you again. What are you doing here with us?" Fin asked, turning to look at the haltia.

Seldrin sighed and crossed his arms in thought. It was clear to Fin that the general was resistant to the question.

"That's why I don't trust people like you, general," Fin said venomously. "There's always a hidden slant, and it's usually one that screws over the honest actors at the worst possible moment."

"Hypocrite," Seldrin replied.

"Oh, do tell," Fin goaded. "Please, judge me from your pedestal. Tell me what an unscrupulous rogue I am."

Seldrin pinched the bridge of his nose. "I won't deny that that's exactly what I think you are, Fin. I've seen many lawbreakers in my time. You fit the mold of quite a few I've sent to the oubliette."

"The fucking oubliette," Fin spat. "*You would* think that's an appropriate punishment for someone like me for simply existing in the same world as you."

Seldrin nodded. "For rapists, murderers, and treasonous bastards? Yes."

"Only two of those things I am, and I say if you're going to sentence a man to death, you kill him clean and outright, not string him up or cram him in a hole and leave him there to die slowly. Only mentally stunted *fucks* with a sick sense of justice think that's an appropriate due for a crime for something like, *oh, I don't know*, taking down a crime lord that's got a mark on you, or offing a king that's committing genocide."

Fin was working himself up. Seldrin was about to respond, but Fin had more to say, leaning back into the man. "And let me tell you, if you think an excruciating death is *just dues* to traitors, then what are you doing here with us? Surely you know the Kingsmen are seeking retribution and recompense against neighboring kingdoms. This work we're embarking on is treason to *some* state. You're probably so simple-minded as to think that if it's your side committing those actions, it's completely justified. Things *aren't* that black and white, soldier boy. In the real world, there's plenty of gray, even within individuals."

"And you say I'm the one on a pedestal preaching?" Seldrin scoffed, shaking his head.

Fin calmed himself. "Alright then. Perhaps I am lumping you into a stereotype. Tell me how I'm wrong about you—and more importantly, answer the damned question; why are you here and not back in Silver Crowns?"

Seldrin was silent for a few moments. He took a seat on the stone bench next to Fin, elbows on his knees in thought. "I think Reza could be right about the White Cloaks pulling strings across the region. I think my people have bought into it, or are at least too scared to address it," he said and sat up straight, almost as if it were a confession he had just gotten off his chest.

"Go on," Fin prompted after a few moments, wanting more from the man than just a vague generalization.

Seldrin looked at Fin, hard-jawed, unsure if he should expound upon his thoughts with someone who had such open distaste for him. In the end, he shrugged, giving in. He didn't see the harm in further explaining his position to Fin. "I have seen corruption in the state's system over the last year or two. Changes that pointed toward favoritism for the church of

Elendium. Rosewood should have been investigated upon its establishment. Instead, officials made special exceptions. Any cases I processed involving White Cloaks or general lay clergy of the church were expedited or dismissed outright—"

He paused, looking to Fin, figuring the man was bound to interrupt him once more with personal attacks. Fin, however, was genuinely listening to him, perhaps for the first time since their meeting.

"When I found Reza and those abused girls at Rosewood, it was clear misdeeds were taking place, and the White Cloaks were involved. To see the case get so turned on its head and for Reza and Kaia to be the ones declared at fault...well, that gave me pause. Enough so that I'm here trying to find out what I can about what's driving this systemic corruption."

Fin let the confession sit for a moment. He looked back out into the twilight forest.

Seldrin tossed his hands up. "Look, I'm going to be honest. I'm not sure the Lost King and his band have the answers I'm looking for. In fact, I still think that they're little more than a band of slighted vigilantes. But I'm reserving that judgment until our meeting with the king himself. I'm hoping to find convincing evidence."

"And if Reza is right, if there is mass manipulation of power across multiple kingdoms by this cult, what then?" Fin replied.

"Well at the least, I'm not going to take part in

the degradation and takeover of the four kingdoms by these White Cloaks. I'll present a case to the High Judges and make a motion for change. If they don't listen, I won't serve as general of the Silver Crowns military anymore," Seldrin answered, his voice dour.

Fin was quiet.

To Seldrin, it seemed that Fin had not been expecting his response and reasoning about why he was there. Perhaps a show of conscience had been out of the question for why the military man had decided to join their group. He hoped that it was one of the few answers that Fin could allow himself to respect.

"And you tagging along with us has nothing to do with getting close to Reza?" Fin asked.

"I wouldn't give up a decorated and hard-fought military career for a *piece of ass.*"

"*That's what they all say*, until it happens," Fin murmured, standing up. Walking back into the guest house, he added, "She's taken, mate. You'd better be good on your word."

The sun was nearly down. What light there was in the gardens was coming from the interior of the castle and its parapets. Seldrin remained on the bench, alone, thinking over Fin's words.

It wasn't long before he heard footsteps on the stone walkway, entering into the gardens. It was not Fin's nimble tread. He guessed it to be Reza walking down the garden path.

She was tentative in her approach, he could sense.

"Seldrin," she called. "Mind if I join you?"

"Please do," he replied.

She took a seat next to him and looked out over the dark horizon, stars beginning to speckle across the night sky.

"Feeling better after all that napping, I hope," Seldrin remarked with a glance at her face. A bruise was quite prominent along her hairline.

"I think so—yes," she said unconvincingly. "At least I feel like I'm not getting worse at this point. It was a bit frightening yesterday. I didn't know where I was headed or how serious my condition was going to get."

"I suppose it's a hidden blessing that the king is taking his sweet time organizing a meeting with us. It seemed you, Kaia, and that *foreigner* needed a day off your feet for once."

"Nomad," Reza corrected firmly.

"Yes." Seldrin chuckled. "Fitting name for that one."

"He's a good man," she defensively censured. "I won't have you, or anyone, belittle him just because he's from a distant land."

"Easy, I meant no harm," Seldrin said. After a few moments of awkward silence, he asked, "So that's the man you were attempting to rush back to at Rosewood?"

"Yes."

"How did he find you? We were on the move constantly," Seldrin asked curiously. "I know for a fact he didn't follow our trail. I would have picked up on that."

"Fin found him, then he found me."

"That man..." Seldrin sighed.

"What about *that man*?" Reza snipped back.

"I don't know how you ended up with the company you did," he said, resting his chin on his hand.

"I keep company with some of the highest caliber of people I've ever met. The way you talk about them, you make it seem like they're below me." She paused, reflecting upon her dear friends that had remained at her side throughout the years. "I'll be completely honest with you—*I'm* beneath them in many regards. It's taken me a good number of hard lessons in humility to force myself to admit it, but I'm lucky they deem me worthy of their company. I don't know what I'd be doing without them."

Seldrin didn't buy it. If Fin was an indicator of the caliber of character she associated with, he doubted the repute of her other associates. "You'd likely be a lot less burdened to advance in your order; I could guarantee you that."

"Perhaps, but to what end?"

"Don't you worship Sareth? Would she not be happy for your support and leadership in her ranks?"

"I...maybe." Reza gave the thought some honest consideration. "I know this may sound like blasphemy to some, but I don't know that her approval of me is the most important thing in my life."

Seldrin was surprised but held his peace as Reza continued.

"It's strange, but I feel that if she does love and care for me, as I think she does, she'd rather I first and foremost be happy in this life—to seek after what truly fulfills me rather than put my whole life's focus into serving her. That doesn't mean I don't serve her with heart and passion, but...of late, I've been seeking fulfillment in ways that feel right to me, which don't directly relate to my faith."

"Well, you certainly are a saren like none I've met before, Reza Malay." Seldrin smiled, leaning back in a stretch with hands behind his head. "I don't know how to reply to that. I'll just say, I wish you luck in your search for purpose. It seems like you have a path you believe in, which is more than most have."

Seldrin turned around abruptly, prompting Reza to follow his gaze. Footsteps tapped along the stone pathway as someone rushed into the garden.

Fin rounded the bend. "Reza, Seldrin, the king is on his way to meet with us. We need you both inside, now."

"Why so sudden? He's coming to us?" Seldrin asked.

"A large coalition of Black Steel and Golden Crown forces are headed this way. Much too large to confront head-on. He's coming to continue the discussion of potential alliances I had started with his son yesterday," Fin explained. "Come. We'll need you both for these talks."

Seldrin stood and offered Reza a hand up. The two rushed inside, following close behind Fin.

The day of rest had come to a sudden end. They all could feel that was the last true rest they would be afforded for a long while.

CHAPTER 23 - PLANS OF THE FIREBRANDS

"Make ready; mind yourselves—the king approaches," Josiah announced as Fin, Reza, and Seldrin entered the gallery.

They had barely returned when four armed soldiers marched into the gallery where they were staying and stationed themselves around the room. The king and his son arrived moments later.

Though neither Fin, Reza, nor any in their company had met the king, they all correctly recognized the regal accouterments and demeanor of royalty.

Johnathan, next to his father, appeared like a mirror in time. The same hard, rough features that defined the warlord's countenance were clearly inherited from his father's stern visage. The brow and grooved age lines showed the capacity to withstand untold hardships associated with lordship, which his muted dark blue and gold robes only accented, topped by a golden crown, replete with sapphires and smoky quartz that seemed to sparkle with starlight. Though

Johnathan's hair was crow black, the king's was peppered, streaked with signs of silver, showing that he was a man past his youthful days but not taken by old age quite yet.

Josiah took a knee upon the king's arrival, and all others followed suit.

"Rise," the Lost King ordered, placing a hand on his son's shoulder. "Welcome to Shadowcliff Castle, Fin and company. I am King Garen Waldock, the true king of the Black Steel Crowns kingdom. I wish we had more time to go over introductions, but time is against us. Johnathan spoke with me about the talk he had with you, Fin of the Plainstate. We have a pressing need to inquire further into the strength of the connections you alluded to. A situation has arisen, which I'll allow Johnathan to give a brief report on before we begin talks of proposals and potential alliances."

Johnathan took a step forward. "I'm under the assumption that most of you understand the dire state the Crowned Kingdoms is currently in as a result of the cult known as the White Cloaks. I'll quickly recap key points to ensure we're all on the same page. I'll speak with you in further detail, Fin, afterward, if there are any further questions."

Fin acknowledged Johnathan with a nod, and the rest of the group made themselves comfortable.

"Five years ago, my father, the rightful king of the Black Steel Crowns kingdom, was dethroned and retreated here to Shadowcliff Castle. Over the next few years, our force withstood attacks from the queen's army; however, it was clear by the numbers she sent that we were not her primary focus. A full-on siege would have easily seen us driven from the land. We established a network of spies and found that the queen was not alone in her designs.

"A cult had been established. Of their origins and formation, we have very little information, but we learned that it was a religious group that worshiped a figure they called Umbraz. Later, this group came to be known as the White Cloaks. It became apparent that the ambition of this cult was insatiable. They spread out through the kingdoms, even to the Southern Sands.

"The cult appeared to attach itself to the faith of Elendium. Again, we do not have timelines on when this connection in the faith occurred, but the Umbraz faith successfully grafted in with the Elendium leadership and began to manipulate both followers and networks and connections that the church of Elendium had established.

"With the Golden Crowns kingdom being the center of Elendium worship, we feared their influence would corrupt the whole kingdom, and sure enough, it did.

"We received reports that a force has amassed to the north in Ash Hollows. The force consists mostly of Black Steel Crowns, but a detachment of Golden

Crown cavalry joined them—likely taking the old trade bridges to the north to stay hidden from us until now. Our scouts reported that the contingent is battle ready and are currently in the process of moving out, coming south. We're the only potential target for such a force, and with the increase in probing attacks the last few days, we fear the worst—that they are headed here to wipe us out.

"Their contingent is sizable and too large to repel or defend against. Our scouts estimate a force of two thousand: Golden Crown cavalry and Black Steel Crown infantry, supported by a number of White Cloak cultists. We have but four hundred soldiers in our ranks. Though our men are loyal, fierce, and well-trained, it would be a slaughter if we stood our ground here, even with the advantage of fortifications and superior skill on the battlefield.

"They should be arriving here within the next day, depending on the urgency of their marching orders."

The king patted his son's shoulder, indicating he'd take it from there. "It is a pressing time, I understand, for all in the kingdoms. The Umbraz cult has proven to be an insidious organization both in battle and in disrupting power structures. Some in their ranks, known as Torchbearers, have supernatural powers—ones that warp and mutate flesh at will. We are struggling to find a counter to their mysterious capabilities. If their numbers and territories continue to grow, and those opposed to this destructive cult do not soon band together, I worry that there will be one faith and one people— the followers of Umbraz. And from what we've seen, Umbraz is not a loving god. There is a genocide in effect, and it will continue to worsen until all are under this cult's thumb or wiped from the face of this land."

The mood in the room, though tense before, now was dire. Reza and the others had been separated from each other for some time, and though each had pieces to the puzzle of the state of the Crowned Kingdoms, they had yet to see the full picture defined so clearly. It lined up with what each had seen individually, making the stakes that much grimmer. Silence shrouded the room as each considered what should now be done to help prevent the doomed scenario from unfolding.

After allowing all in the room to absorb his words, the king spoke once more. "Fin, I need to know if your talks of diplomacy are honest."

Fin nodded his understanding. The king and his son had laid out their predicament and needs very clearly, and he well understood the corruption of Umbraz.

"Perhaps going over a list of potential support would be prudent," Fin said, rubbing his stubble. "I do not speak for all the connections I mentioned last night. Reza and Kaia would be better speakers for the saren order, and General Seldrin would best represent the Silver Crowns kingdom."

Reza looked to Fin, then to the king, seeing the prompt from both to answer as the representative for her people. She cleared her throat. "West Perch is a smaller monastery, but there are saren knights, priestesses, and a high priestess that would likely come to aid a just resistance effort or harbor as many of your people as they could. I know West Perch would not be capable of housing your full force, but perhaps the Castle Sephentho south of there could take the rest. They have worked together in the past."

"Kaia"—Reza turned to the younger saren —"what do you think West Perch's stance would be?"

"West Perch is selective in their involvement within the kingdoms," she said in a quiet, controlled tone. "I am on their board and have some sway with the sisterhood council. I could try to present your case and see if support and aid could be granted. Though I cannot promise a favorable outcome, I can promise you that I will do everything in my power to ensure that they understand the situation and advocate for action."

"That would be appreciated," the king replied, a small smile gracing his features.

His attention then turned to General Seldrin.

Seldrin took a moment to consider the request, folding his arms and sighing before explaining, "My being here was unexpected. I was on a different mission completely when I fell in with Reza and her crew. This is quite a bit to absorb, if I am to speak candidly. Explaining what I've learned of the White Cloaks alone will tax the limits of my reach within the Silver Crowns government, let alone act in a diplomatic capacity between your clan and my people. I'm not convinced Silver Crowns would be your best option for refuge. I'm not saying that I wouldn't help facilitate talks, but I think it should be considered a last option—not a first."

The king's demeanor turned hard, but he nodded his understanding of the general's position and seemed to appreciate the honesty.

Fin once again addressed the king to speak for his own ties. "I truly only represent one potential connection, the Plainstate. Reza and Nomad share a similar claim to authority with that state. Sultan Metus is the most just ruler I've ever had the privilege of serving. I have full faith that he'd be willing to agree to resettle your people. He may even help support a coalition if we can unify against the Umbraz movement. But the Plainstate is far to the south. It may be impractical to expect full support from them so far away, even if they are willing to help."

The king and his son did not seem hopeful. Seeing their disappointment, Fin held up a hand to stave off their comments. "The other connection I have is with Marshal Reid, currently leading the Rediron kingdom to a path of recovery from the devastating warp. We now know that the warp sickness was a man-made sickness synthesized and disseminated by the White Cloaks. I believe Marshal Reid is a good man. I think he would understand your situation and perhaps even support forming an alliance."

"I see," the king mused. He rubbed his peppered beard. "This could work in the favor of the realm. Our situation could act as a rallying signal for the surrounding kingdoms. I do not see any of us being successful alone in combating the White Cloaks, but together, perhaps we can root out Umbraz's corrupting influence and banish his followers from the Crowned Kingdoms for good."

"Fin," the king said at length. "Of all the paths forward, I feel this Marshal Reid may be our best option, simply due to proximity. I've had heated contentions with King Maxim the whole of my reign. Our kingdoms have not been on the best of terms. However, if you think this Marshal is a better man than Maxim, I believe we both have suffered at the hands of the same enemy. Unity against a common foe often provides fertile ground for strong alliances. Perhaps we should start there, making for Castle Sauvignon in Rediron, and enter talks of forming a resistance force against the White Cloaks."

"I agree," Fin said. "It seems a natural fit."

"I do not trust Alumin," the king continued. "Our chapter there has been giving us worrying reports that the bureaucracy has taken a turn for the worse."

"It is effectively a church-run state at this point," Fin chipped in.

"It would be best to use the old roads to the south, sire," Johnathan suggested. "We should not use the highway that runs through Alumin, there's too much risk of getting involved with a potentially hostile Alumin guard weaponized by the church. Their city-state alone boasts six hundred city guards. Even half of that would be enough to cause considerable trouble for us if we're also contending with the queen's force pursuing our flank."

"If I may, your highness," Kaia said softly, garnering everyone's attention. "If I am to speak with the sisterhood at West Perch, then I would need to part ways with everyone now if you do indeed intend to march southwards to Rediron instead of using the main highway."

"That sounds sensible," the king agreed.

"I will send a two-man detachment to escort her there," Johnathan offered.

"That will not be necessary. With my hip still healing, I'll not be much good on the warpath in your company for a while yet. I'll go with her," Nomad insisted, drawing attention from the warlord who was clearly not used to being contested over orders. The two did not seem pleased with the interruption. Nomad attempted to explain. "Forgive me, Warlord Waldock, but I do not know your two men, and I do not know you. I insist on accompanying the young lady."

The warlord eyed the foreigner for a moment but relented the point. "So be it. We will provide you with horses. I would appreciate a report once the sisterhood has made a decision."

"I will return once an answer has been made," Nomad said, bowing his head in appreciation.

"I will join you both, at least till West Perch," Seldrin said. "I should have no issues on the highways returning to Silver Crowns. I'll call a council with the heads of state and put forth a motion to support Rediron and your warband."

Fin leaned in and whispered to Reza, "Looks like that leaves just you and me heading back to Rediron."

"Once in Rediron, I'll need to return to High Cliffs Monastery," Reza said, seeing the roles forming up now. "Lanereth and the others need to know about all this. High Cliffs may join the war effort. They'll be able to send word to the Plainstate and update the other surrounding territories of the threat of Umbraz. It would be best to get word out to as many trusted territories as possible down south. There may be sympathetic parties willing to help."

"That would be most helpful." The king gave a slight bow of his head. "We would be in your debt."

The king waited to see if there were any further suggestions before concluding. "There's plenty of logistics and preparations to see to. We'll give you all time to discuss your plans. I'll send three horses for Kaia, General Seldrin, and Nomad. Reza and Fin, we'll reconvene with you after that. You'll travel with us at the head of the troop as special counsel and envoys if you are agreeable to that."

"That'll be fine," Fin consented. "And time to discuss all of this alone would be appreciated, thank you."

"We'll leave you to it," Johnathan announced, gesturing to the four Kingsguard to be ready to move out.

"May your respective gods remember the kindness you showed us this day and watch over you on your travels," the king said. "I will not forget that you were among the first to stand by me and my son in our time of need."

"Take care this night," Johnathan told Seldrin, Kaia, and Nomad, then turned to Nomad and Reza. "We'll return later for you. Be ready to head out with us."

Fin and Reza nodded solemnly, and the Kingsguard moved out with the king and Johnathan following up the rear of the formation.

Their armored footsteps were soon distant, and then the front door closed, leaving Reza and the others in silence in the dim, empty guest wing.

They had each been swept up in the sudden fervor of the moment, all volunteering to participate in no simple task. Now, the reality of the effort began to settle in.

"This could be the start of a war," Kaia said.

"It most certainly could be," Fin agreed.

The room was quiet once more.

Lines of an old haltia soldier's poem came to Seldrin's mind and all listened as he spoke them aloud:

"The end of peace, of youth, of life,

The beginning of death, of rot, of strife,

Many will perish, few will remain,

But none, in war, will ever be the same."

CHAPTER 24 - FAREWELLS

Fog rolled in as the night waxed on, obscuring the star and moonlight, promising to give troubles to the three on the trail as they finished packing their things onto the fresh mounts provided them by the Kingsmen.

Seldrin was up on his steed first, checking his saber, bow, and trail equipment once over, anxious to hit the road before the fog got any worse.

Kaia gave Reza a hug, lingering in her embrace. Reza smiled and patted her back. Letting go, Kaia bowed to Fin with a nervous smile, excited, albeit slightly scared, to be a part of the monumental effort that likely would go down in the Crowned Kingdom's history books. She hopped up on her speckled mare and nudged up to Seldrin's mount.

"A moment, please," Nomad said to Kaia and Seldrin. Taking Reza's hand, he led her a little ways off, rubbing her hand with his thumb.

Nomad came to a stop once they were out of sight of the others. He lifted her hand and kissed it tenderly. "We did not get much time together." His quiet voice was softened by the fog.

"We did not," she lamented, taking both his hands in hers now.

"I'll take care of Kaia, ensure that she's escorted safely, and that your order listens to her. I'll reconnect with you in Rediron when I can."

"See that you do, please," she said, her eyes locked on their gently swaying hands. "And Nomad —" she added. "I've been meaning to tell you something..."

He patiently waited for her to find the words she struggled to voice, his eyes lovingly looking over her features.

"I'm sorry. I should have been better to you these last few months. I let frustrations get the better of me, and—I don't know—I get *so angry* at times with the structure of my order. You didn't deserve what I put you through those long weeks in Alumin. I'm sorry, I'll be better, I promise—"

Nomad tugged on her hands, pulling her in. Their lips met, quieting her as they kissed, concealed from sight by the fog.

They shared breath for a few long moments before Nomad let her go. "I loved you then, and I love you now."

A sudden tear lined her eye. Her smile only brightened his own.

"There's that smile. It can be matched by no other," he warmly crooned.

Embracing her fondly once more, he whispered in her ear through her platinum locks. "You brought me back to this life, and you are why I decided to stay a while longer."

She squeezed him tight, nuzzling into the crook of his shoulder, lingering on the feeling of him for as long as he allowed her.

After a time, they walked back into the courtyard, holding hands.

Fin smiled at the two. He appreciated how far they had come from the first time they all met in the Southern Sands years ago.

Nomad clapped a hearty arm around Fin and gave him a warm smile as he jumped up into his horse's saddle.

The three settled in atop their mounts as Reza came back into the torch glow in the courtyard, wiping fresh tears but smiling as she stood next to Fin to see their friends off.

"Take care of each other," Fin called.

"No need to worry, I'll see that they behave," Kaia returned, smiling back as the three snapped the reins to start the horses down the cobblestone road that led them out of the castle courtyard and back to the paths to West Perch and Alumin.

Reza and Fin stood out in the fog for a few minutes more after the trio had vanished into the cloud, silent in each other's company.

"Oh, Fin," Reza breathed, holding a hand up to her mouth.

"I know," was all he could say to comfort her, pulling her in, arm over her shoulder. "I know."

CHAPTER 25 - CHAOS IN THE COURTYARD

"You've secured the treasury?" the king asked Johnathan as they rode into the guest wing's courtyard.

"Treasury and the high-value items from the armory were packed up and stowed on four light wagons. They're with second company."

"What about provisions?"

"Third company."

Hearing the king's company approach, Fin and Reza walked out of the guest wing's double doors to greet them.

"Hail, King Waldock." Fin announced his and Reza's presence with an open hand.

"Hail, Fin—Reza," the king greeted. "Looks as though your company has left for the trail back to Alumin?"

Fin nodded. "They left a few hours ago."

The king nodded in return, satisfied that all was

settled on Fin's end. He turned to talk with Johnathan again. "I suppose most of our force has seen to the transport of all that we can reasonably take with us? All that's left is waiting for the scouts to return and report."

"The scouts have not reported back yet," said Johnathan. "They should have by now..."

There was an unnerving calm and silence for a moment. Johnathan looked out into the featureless fogbank that settled upon the castle grounds. "We'll need to leave the castle soon. We've delayed longer than I had wished in waiting for their return. It is not safe to linger here with only the Kingsguard. They're our top soldiers, but they still only number twelve. We need to catch up to all companies within the hour, my liege."

One of the Kingsguard led two horses up for Reza and Fin to start loading their stuff onto. Both worked quickly to pack their things on their respective mounts, but the silence in the court was bordering on eerie, and the fog dampened what little sound that was made.

"Sire, we should be off to rejoin the rest of the host," one of the Kingsguard said respectfully.

Johnathan was about to speak when a thump from elsewhere in the courtyard silenced them all.

Johnathan made a quick motion, holding up three fingers, pointing to his eyes, then pointed in the direction of the sound. Three Kingsguard dismounted with hardly a sound and were stalking in the direction of the noise within moments. Two swords unsheathed. The bowman nocked an arrow as they advanced into the fog bank.

Both Fin and Reza checked their weapon hilts as everyone in the foggy courtyard waited in bated silence. It didn't take long.

All could make out a frantic rustle of chainmail and a call to arms from one of the guardsmen. Johnathan and four guards dismounted swiftly, moving in to provide backup, multiple swords now out and gleaming fiery orange in the torchlight.

Fin made a move to follow suit. Reza cinched her last bag to the horse and followed Fin to the first sounds of battle—steel striking steel.

Reza could see Johnathan up ahead at the edge of her vision. He was barking out commands now. A Kingsguard hauled a fellow guardsman by the cuirass, pulling him back to where the horses were. The man had been pelted with multiple crossbow bolts, thick-shafted and deeply penetrating layers of armor. The man was no longer moving.

She looked to Fin to see his reaction to the sudden, dire situation. He wore a mask of war. No worry, fear, or surprise could be seen in his eyes. It was clear he thought of nothing else but neutralizing the threat. She attempted to slip into the same headspace of combat and survival.

Fin had gotten ahead of her. His knives were

out, and he was now speaking with Johnathan.

Reza saw a figure to her right. A few steps closer and she could see a downed guardsman.

She rushed to his side, took a knee, and flipped him over on his back. Through his chest piece protruded a heavy crossbow bolt, dark red blood staining the ground beneath him. The man was limp in her hands.

She stood up, hearing the click of a crossbow just before the missile cut past her. Reza looked in the direction from which the bolt was fired. She could see figures along the courtyard wall, repositioning, cranking and reloading crossbows. She moved to retreat to Fin and Johnathan when a sword swung at her. Bringing up her longsword just in time to deflect the attack, she stepped back. A golden-armored knight lunged up to her with another swing of his bastard sword.

She deflected again, ready this time to change angles to stab at the knight's face and neck in return. The knight sidestepped and slapped her blade hard on the flat with a single-handed battle axe. A regular sword would have easily been snapped by the blow, but Reza's meteorite blade was a masterwork in the craft of bladesmithing. It absorbed the blow without showing even a bend or crack.

She withdrew and stabbed toward the face of the knight once more, her sword's greater length giving her an advantage as she pressed the knight back a step.

Another few clicks from crossbows upon the wall sent her diving and scrambling blindly, determined not to be an easy target for her foes. She came up out of a roll, having avoided two more bolts that skipped angrily off the stone floor, but the golden knight rushed her, swinging in hard with his two weapons.

She knew she couldn't take the blows. She sprung backward, turned, and ran toward Fin.

Fin chucked two daggers over her shoulder. One bounced off the knight's helm, and the other dug into the visor around the mouth.

The knight's step faltered but he kept his forward momentum, even with blood now speckling his helmet and a dagger hilt protruding from the slits in his visor.

"Guards, fall back! Archers, covering fire! They're up on the wall!" Johnathan barked, leading a few guards steadily back toward the king.

Reza met up with Fin. Another guard plowed violently into the side of the golden knight, sprawling him out on the cobblestone. Reza turned and rushed back to where the horses were.

A giant of a man, nearly as large as the hunchback she had seen in Rosewood, was batting Kingsguard out of the way with an ironwood club on his path toward the king. The club was more the size of a support beam, but the large man wielded it proficiently. Each smash of the club blew apart the Kingsguards' armor. After the front line of guards were splayed out, unconscious or dead across the yard, the last two guards were particularly weary of the giant's range and goaded him by leaping back out of the club's reach as the golden giant struggled to slam the last two soldiers.

Reza rushed up behind the golden-armored brute, thrusting her longsword's tip into the lower back of the giant's chainmail. It broke through links, and though the initial strike only managed to gouge into the man's back, Reza planted her feet and pressed in and up hard, shivving the giant deep, slicing through layers of muscle and shearing vertebrae and rib bone.

The man roared in pain and reflexively thrashed about with his massive club. Though Reza anticipated the move by slicking out the length of her bloodied blade and leaping back, the ironwood club still managed to clip her, sending her to the ground.

The huge golden knight screamed in bloody rage. He turned and stumbled for a moment—locking his gaze on Reza, who was laid out, still reeling as she struggled to get up.

Fin slipped in, sword point stabbing at the large man's face. He dug in through the visor again and again. The knight swatted away the attack, but Fin's sword tip had come back bloodied.

Fin barely dodged the swing of the club and sidestepped out of range, leaving Reza clear in the hulk's path. If he still had sight, she wasn't sure; but as he raised his club high over her, ready to slam her into the ground, she knew it didn't matter.

The king, still mounted, reared up his steed next to the golden knight. Horseshoe hooves banged off the helm of the giant, once, then twice, toppling him and knocking his helmet loose to expose his lacerated face.

Two of Fin's throwing daggers thudded into the giant's face as easily as if his head were a carved pumpkin, one directly after another. This time, the giant slammed to the ground, unmoving.

"King Waldock, we need to ride—now," Fin called over the din of battle that was getting closer to them by the moment. The king was hardly listening, now looking for his son.

Kingsguards were giving ground, returning to the horses that were about ready to bolt.

One of the two Kingsguard screamed in pain suddenly, no sign of bolt or foe nearby. Reza stepped cautiously toward the guard writhing in agony.

His screams halted, turning into a gurgling retching sound before his body began to convulse and ripple. The man's armor bulged, and then split at the seams; the man was ripping out of his own skin, exploding right before Reza's eyes.

Within seconds, the guard was a heap of flesh and armor.

The last guard positioned himself in front of the king as two White Cloaks parted the fog, chanting and holding up the pearls of their god.

A bronze streak of a dagger flew past Reza and pinned into the chest of the closest White Cloak, quickly staining the man's robes red.

Fin stepped up next to Reza and threw another bronze dagger thirty feet at the man still standing, pegging into his shoulder.

The man continued, raising his pearl high, his chanting growing in fervor as he turned his focus from the remaining guard to Fin.

Fin held another bronze throwing dagger in his hand, about to cock back and toss it. He froze up suddenly, the dagger clanging off the ground. He crumpled over, clutching his stomach as the White Cloak centered on Fin with prayer and the power of the pearl exerting its influence over him.

Reza knew the only way to help him now was to kill the man that raised his voice in prayer to Umbraz.

The other White Cloak joined in the assault, speaking blasphemous utterances that filled the courtyard. Fin screamed in pain, curled up in the fetal position.

Reza knew she couldn't make it to the chanting men in time to stop them. She picked up the bronze throwing daggers that Fin had dropped and hurled them as true as she could at the two Torchbearers.

She wasn't skilled with throwing daggers, but fortune favored her aim, and the dagger landed in the supporting Torchbearer's stomach, halting his chant for a moment.

Fin's screams continued as the chants started up again. Reza gave a battle cry and rushed toward the Torchbearers, afraid that by the time she closed the gap, they would have finished their deadly prayer.

A shadow appeared behind the Torchbearer furthest away from Reza. Just as she could make out Johnathan rushing up behind him, the warchief's claymore swung with such force that it slashed through the Torchbearer's midsection. The man doubled over, torso toppling to the ground, severed from his other half.

An arrow from a Kingsguard archer thudded into the remaining Torchbearer's chest. This time, he stopped chanting, gasping for breath, his lung now punctured.

Johnathan chopped down on the man's neck, executioner style.

"On your horse, now," Johnathan called to Reza and Fin as he rushed to his father's side. "Mount up! Protect the king!" he boomed to the rest of the remaining company, ordering a retreat.

"Fin, wake up!" Reza cried, shaking him in her

arms.

Guardsmen ran past them, heeding the order to mount and encircle the king. Johnathan was calling out more commands to his people, but Reza was hardly concerned with anyone but Fin.

She sheathed her sword and scooped him up, starting back toward their horses. Johnathan was no longer in the courtyard, or at least he wasn't visible through the fog. She could still hear his calls, but they were distant, the company in full gallop heading away from them now.

Her and Fin's horses had retreated into the porch of the guest building. With some effort, she got Fin up in the saddle of her horse.

A bolt thudded into the door a hand's width away from Reza. She ducked and turned to spot the crossbowman. He was close. Dropping the crossbow on the cobblestone floor, he rushed at her, drawing a shortsword as he closed the gap.

She fumbled for her sword, ready to draw it just before the man made it to her. Her sword never came out of its sheath. An arrow drove straight through the side of the charging man's coiffed head.

One of the Kingsguard archers ran up to her.

"Come," the woman whispered. "We're dead if we stay here. Ten more sun warriors just entered the yard."

Reza mounted up behind Fin, holding him snug

to her as the archer mounted Fin's horse next to them.

"We'll head out the back way through the gardens," she said, and led Reza away from the ambush that had decimated the Kingsguard and left Fin unconscious.

CHAPTER 26 - FLIGHT

"Your name, guardswoman," Reza hoarsely whispered to the Kingsguard archer that had led them out of the gardens and through the woodlands just east of the castle grounds.

The rider fell back to trot beside Reza and Fin for a moment, an eye constantly on the watch for danger.

"Cass," she whispered, then looked at Fin who was still slumped over in Reza's arms. "Does he breathe?"

They had come to a stop in the cover of the tree line. Reza took off her glove and pressed her hand against Fin's chest, waiting to feel it rise and fall. After a moment, she felt his rhythm.

"Yes. He breathes," Reza said.

"Riding fast is going to be tricky with you managing him," the guardswoman noted.

A call from the castle alerted them before a torch lit the wall. They stayed still, hoping that they were deep enough in the trees to shroud them in shadows and fog.

"Eastern front, clear!" a man yelled from upon

the wall.

Another man further out shouted, "Eastern force, split! Half of you secure the area and wait for the main host; the other half join the western lightning force and pursue."

"Shit," Cass cursed under her breath. "We need to go now and catch up to the king or we'll be cut off."

"I'll ride as hard as I'm able," Reza assured her, inviting Cass to lead them out of the thickets and into the ruins at the edge of the castle's perimeter.

Cass did not stop to look back. Reza struggled to maneuver the winding streets and keep pace with her within the first minute of bolting from the woods. The fog was slightly lighter as they raced out onto the road past the ruins, and Cass found the trail their company had taken when retreating southwards earlier that night.

Reza glanced back as the sound of horse hooves neared from behind. The fog still obscured how many riders followed in pursuit. She had no idea if the enemy pursued her or was simply on the same trail tracking the retreating Kingsmen, hoping to harry any lagging troops. It didn't matter, for they were fast gaining upon her.

Cass had well outpaced Reza. There was nothing to be done about that. With both Reza and Fin's weight, her horse was already at a disadvantage. On top of that, riding at a full gallop risked jostling Fin or losing her grip on him.

She turned off along the path to a road freshly trampled by hundreds of horses, hoping that she was headed in the right direction.

A noise ahead cautioned her to slow down. The dirt trail ended, leading out into a meadow. The noise of a downpour came rushing in as a gray sheet of rain closed in on them.

The deluge shot chills up her spine, taking her breath away as the horse whinnied. With a start, Fin nodded awake at the cold, pelting rain. He yelled out in pain, clutching at his head as Reza tried to juggle him and still keep her focus on the trail.

Reza called Fin's name through the pouring rain. It was clear his head was killing him. The color drained from her as she considered the possibility that one of the White Cloaks could have warped the inside of his head, even if the zealot hadn't had the time to finish his incantation and flower his brain until it burst from his skull.

"Hang in there!" she shouted, but Fin was much too absorbed with grunting through waves of excruciating pain to hear her.

The glint of gold in her peripheral warned Reza that they were not alone in the muddy field. More Golden Knights rode hard at her other flank, coming up to pincer in on Reza's heaving horse. The mounting feeling that it would only be a matter of moments before a spear would lance her through the back pervaded her every thought.

Through the rain ahead, she saw more figures—many more. For a brief moment, she worried that the Golden Crown knights had somehow gotten ahead of her and were forming a line to stop her, but as she rode closer, she could see Kingsmen galloping her way. A line of nearly a hundred armed soldiers raced toward the enemy's lightning force that had overextended themselves in giving chase to a single foe.

The Kingsmen's forces were on the lightning force too quick for an about-face. Impact and the crash of steel and flesh sounded on the battlefield behind Reza as she tried to slow her heaving horse. Fin's writhing made it impossibly hard to manage the reins.

She dismounted, battle cries and the sound of combat not too far behind her. She lowered Fin into the wet grass, hunching over him to keep the rain from pelting into his pain-wracked face. He was thrashing so terribly that she was forced to hold his face in her hands in an effort to reach through to him. She cried his name but could see that he was not in a state to comprehend her.

She knew what she had to do. She needed to perform another healing on him. Without knowing how much internal damage had been done, or even the nature of the infliction Fin struggled with now, she could be jumping into an incurable condition. If his brain had indeed been scrambled and deformed beyond hope, then even exposing herself to such trauma could create a fatal sink of aether, completely wipe her out or even cause lasting damage to herself. To actually attempt to heal such a fatal flaw would be a fool's errand.

"Fin. I have to try. I'm sorry," she said over the din of the rain.

He was weeping now, the pain overwhelming him. Her tears mingled with his as she touched his forehead with hers, holding his head in her hands. She reached deep within and said a quick prayer to Sareth, entering the stream of aether that linked her spirit to Fin's.

"My lords! We found them," a soldier called out to the warchief and king.

Johnathan dismounted, joined by Cass that had rushed ahead of Reza and Fin to announce to the warchief of the lightning force's pursuit. Thankfully, they had been able to connect with the rearguard company.

They came quickly to where Reza and Fin lay, crumpled in the tall, wet grass. Their horse lay next to them, heaving. The warchief rushed to their side and snapped for a nearby soldier to see to their horse.

"Josiah, Cass," Johnathan said, brushing the hair from Reza's face and checking for her pulse just under her jaw. "See to these two. I'll not have them die like this," he said in an almost tender tone that both soldiers had rarely heard.

"Yes, my lord," both replied, moving to lift Fin and Reza from their nest of grass.

Johnathan slammed his gauntleted fist into the ground, relieving a jolt of frustration over the execution of the evening's tradeoffs.

The two guards halted for a moment as they heard the warchief admit under his breath, "Our very kingdom now depends on them."

CHAPTER 27
- AWAKE

Amber light filtered into the small, slitted windows, causing Reza to wince in annoyance as the evening sun found her eyelids. Rousing after finding no solace from the sun's rays, she sat up, rubbing her face, letting out a long yawn.

She looked around the small room in a daze, for a moment confused at her surroundings. Then, with a jolt, she recalled her last conscious moments before waking up alone in a castle bedchamber—she had found holes in Fin's skull.

"Oh my god. Fin," she breathed, thinking back on the moments before unconsciousness.

The initial connection had been a shock, absorbing her whole self into the healing. She had known from the start she only had a matter of moments before going unconscious—and she knew it would not be enough to save Fin.

She had tried to patch one hole, but already, the darkness was taking over. She had just started to fade off when a warm white light rushed down through her head and into her chest, filling her with just enough aether to work on the next hole—and the next.

She had blacked out at some point—she couldn't remember if she had completed the healing or not.

She had prayed to Sareth before beginning the blessing...had Sareth heard her prayer?

Sareth had been a very distant heavenly mother all Reza's life. Reza had only ever had a handful of moments that she could say were spiritual. She wasn't entirely sure that the warmth that she felt was Sareth, but she couldn't think of what else it might have been. The warmth was comforting, loving—fierce.

Thinking over the experience a while longer, she decided that she needed to find Fin and figure out where she was. She went to stand up a little too hastily and toppled out of the bed and onto the floor like a newborn pup, a tangled heap of blankets and limbs.

She was struggling to unwrap herself from the mess, sitting up on the hardwood floor, when a vaguely familiar voice called to her on the other side of the door.

"Reza, are you alright?" Cass cracked the door open and peered in.

Reza cursed, embarrassed by the mess she was in, feeling so weak that it was making getting herself sorted from the blankets a real struggle.

"Let me help you with that," Cass remarked, moving to help Reza to sit up on the bedside, sitting next to her.

"You've been out a while. Was worried you weren't going to make it," Cass said as she kept a steadying hand on Reza's shoulder.

Though Reza had endured comas before, never were they not a worrying sign for her. She took a moment to utter a brief prayer to her goddess in thanks for helping her to pull through another one.

"Where are we?" Reza asked, a hand holding the side of her head to stop things from spinning.

"In the Sauvignon barracks," Cass said. "In Rediron country."

"We made it then," Reza sighed, feeling a weight lift from her.

"We did." Cass offered a small smile. "Though it was close. We did lose a number of soldiers—eighteen as far as we've counted."

"I'm sorry to hear that," Reza offered, knowing full well the unspoken hardships of losing any member of a company.

Cass nodded. "Could have been much worse if you and your friend Fin had not suggested beginning talks with King Reid."

"Where's Fin now?"

"I'm not sure," Cass admitted. "He was here. The barracks is at full capacity with no bed to spare. You two were sharing this room. This afternoon he vanished. Josiah can't even find him, and he was strictly tasked to stick with him."

"Are you tasked to stick with me?"

Cass nodded.

"Well, I'm starving," Reza sighed, rubbing her grumbling stomach. "Mind if we see if there's anything to eat at the mess hall?"

Cass nodded, moving to stand up. "Sure, we can do that. I'll warn you, slim pickings since we got here. Housing and feeding an extra four hundred soldiers is putting a bit of stress on the Redironers. Our food supplies were scant due to having so little time to pick up before being ordered to head out. We didn't bring much with us."

Reza yawned. "As long as it's edible, I don't care. Bread, cheese, and water would do."

"I think we can do a bit better than that." Cass smiled, helping Reza to her feet. "Here, let's get you up and moving."

Unsteady at first, Reza leaned on Cass as they navigated the narrow halls and down a flight of stairs to the mess hall.

The room was packed and making their way to the serving counter took an exhausting amount of effort. By the time they both had food and went to find a table, Reza was beginning to feel uneasy in the crowded space, tired, hungry, and thirsty.

"So, the last thing I remember was performing

a healing on Fin, then..." Reza started as they sat down at one of the few empty tables. "Did the Golden Knights give chase for much longer?"

Cass sighed, recalling the dark night of flight where she and her comrades abandoned their home. It had been a difficult couple of days for the Kingsmen. She buttered a roll and began to explain. "The scouting force was handled easily enough. Their fifteen to our hundred rearguard were promptly handled, even before any could retreat. However, a larger cavalry unit of Golden Crowns and White Cloaks gave chase after that. We were just heading up the old roads at the border of the Salen Greenwood forest when the fog and rain cleared, and we spotted their cavalry far across the open field from whence we had come. We began to double time over the old hunting trails at the risk of losing our way."

"What happened to the scouts that we had been waiting for at the castle that night?" Reza asked.

Cass shook her head grimly. "They're numbered in the eighteen missing. Likely captured or killed."

Reza paused from eating her meal, truly sad to hear the news. Scouts, spies, and assassins usually got the worst treatment when it came to being prisoners of war.

"May that not be the case," Reza whispered.

Cass did not seem to share her optimism. "We traversed the woods through the night, and their archers did give our flank trouble. We ended up taking a few casualties from their harassment, but by the time they had come within lancing range, we had broken through the south side of the Greenwood.

"Sunrise had come on by then, and Dunnmur city guardsmen had spotted the force early on and mobilized as we rushed southward. Dunnmur's minute men only consisted of a hundred cavalry archers, but it was enough to give the pursuing Golden Crowns pause.

"There was a brief standoff, likely their commander assessing the odds, but more Dunnmur troops had been trickling out of the city gates to support their flash force. The Golden Crowns and the White Cloaks rode back north through the woods."

Reza had resumed her feast. "What did the Dunnmur militia do then?"

"Well, not that they could really do anything; we outnumbered them after all," Cass chuffed. "Their commanding officer came to speak with the king and Warchief Waldock. Our situation was explained as we held our position until all could be made known to the city mayor. Apparently, they had just had a new mayor instated, so the whole process took most of the day." Cass started on her meal, mentioning as an aside, "Fin awoke around then."

"How was his condition when he awoke?" Reza asked between sips from her water mug.

"He was sluggish, extremely drained, but seemed with it enough," Cass replied, more interested in her meal than talking about Fin. "Josiah was with him all that night. Had a headache that kept him up."

She shifted her tone. "Anyways, from there, it was agreed that they would escort our force southwards through the Nightshade Forest to Sauvignon. The following day we were without the gates of the castle, both lord Waldocks in talks with King Reid. It's been a few days now, and they're still in talks. I think King Reid wishes to absorb our military in turn for taking us in. King Waldock wishes to remain independent. They're having issues seeing eye to eye."

Reza idly looked off into the dining hall, which was packed with both Rediron soldiers and Kingsmen. Though on the surface, she didn't see any spats between the countrymen, she didn't doubt that there was some level of resentment held by both sides. From what little she knew about the two kingdoms, Rediron and Black Steels had a long history of guarded isolationism. She wondered how things were going to pan out between the two groups, especially amongst the leadership.

Cass seemed content with focusing on her food, leaving Reza to her thoughts. The two finished their meals before long. Cass helped Reza to her feet once more and led them out of the busiest room in the barracks.

"Cass," Reza said, pausing to look out the arrow-slit window as they headed back up the stairs to her bedroom. "Mind if we head to the roof? I'd like to see if there's a view from a lookout above. I've never been to Sauvignon. I'd like to get a look of the countryside before the sun goes down."

Nodding, Cass took her past her room and up another flight of stairs. She assisted her up a short ladder to a hatch that led out onto the roof. A Rediron watchman helped her and Cass up; after exchanging some pleasantries, he led them over to the lookout point.

Cass allowed Reza a moment to herself. She returned to the bench by the hatch and struck up a conversation with the Rediron watchman. Reza watched them for a moment, then turned and leaned against the low stone wall along the buttressed lookout point, taking in the scene of the city of Sauvignon that was bathed in sunset hues.

Though she'd seen little of Rediron country, she was touched by the rustic beauty of the forested hills and mountain ranges. Rediron was a kingdom of the people: farmers, merchants, traders, craftsmen, trappers, and hunters. There was a feeling of quaint solitude within its borders, the exact opposite of Alumin with its great industrial artistry and economy-driven governance.

The sun was just dipping over the horizon of trees far to the west. She could already see torches beginning to light up across the city below. Suddenly, she was overcome with a profound thankfulness that she was alive to witness another sunset.

She had had another extremely close call. She knew Fin, as godless as he was, would mockingly owe all credit of their fortune to his self-conceived *God of Luck*. She, however, wondered if Sareth had been the reason for their continued survival.

She wished she knew where Fin was now. She knew he couldn't have gone far and likely was within city boundaries—somewhere down there amongst the lamp-lit streets.

She worried for him. His healing had been dangerously close to his brain. From what she had learned from Lanereth, brain healings were off-limits, for good reason, amongst saren ministry work. The brain, as with the heart, was an extraordinarily complex structure, and when knitting tissue back together, sarens were rarely met with success, even with the most adept healers among them. She prayed that all had healed properly with Fin. She'd find it hard to believe Sareth would have aided her if she knew the healing wasn't destined to be successful.

She sighed, frustration flaring up. "Wherever you are, scoundrel," she whispered as she looked out into the lively evening streets, "you better have a good reason for disappearing on me."

CHAPTER 28 - CLANDESTINE MEETING WITH THE KING

Little had changed about the marshal's room. Fin considered the fact that Reid could have upgraded his quarters upon being crowned and had chosen not to. The same heirloom sword remained mounted above the hearth, the same brand of brandy on the bar countertop, and the same thin cigars laid out on the coffee table....

It seemed that Reid was a man of old habits and simple pleasures. He kept things practical—familiar. Fin supposed that wasn't a bad thing. A traditional man, one not prone to fanciful whims, might be able to focus on the health of a kingdom rather than chase after his own extravagant passions. Perhaps it was just wishful thinking on his part.

Fin heard footsteps approaching. With Reid's quarters the only ones on this level, he knew who it was who stepped up to the door and fidgeted with the lock. Fin took a seat at the bar and poured himself a glass of brandy, giving the spirit a whiff as Reid opened the door.

"Fin…" Reid seethed. "I told King Waldock that I didn't want to see you anywhere near my castle—"

"*Your* castle?" Fin scoffed. "It's humorous how quickly you fell into the role of a king."

Reid eyed him for a long moment. Fin began to wonder if the man was considering calling the guards over the intrusion. Thankfully, Reid closed the door with a frustrated sigh and snatched up a cigar from his table, striking a match and lighting up. After a few calculating draws from his cigar, he walked around the bar into his kitchen across from Fin and studied the man.

"Last time we talked, you told me, in no uncertain terms, that if you ever had to come back here, you'd see that I lie face down in a pool of my own blood," Reid said gruffly.

"I did say that, didn't I?" Fin replied in all seriousness. Breaking eye contact to take a healthy swig of brandy, he sighed. "Well, that's not my intention now." He poured another glass of brandy and nudged the drink over to Reid. "Here's to your promotion."

Reid's stern face was unrelenting; he didn't even look down at the glass. Fin gave up on the pleasantries. He genuinely did wish to shoot the shit with him, considering their complicated past, but he could see now that his presence only heaped additional problems upon Reid's doorstep—a fact that Reid clearly did not appreciate.

Reid blew a stream of smoke out and smoothed down his thick mustache in thought. "You ain't welcomed here, Fin. Neither is King Waldock and his men. Rediron has barely had time to even find its wounds, let alone begin to nurse them. Half the towns are still coming to terms with what that damnable white spice was and what they can do to reverse its damage. They have a new king to adjust to. The lords accepted my coronation but aren't happy with it and are likely scheming on how to reverse it. We've got plenty of problems ourselves without needing to be thinking of helping a banished king and four hundred loyalists—"

"That's exactly why you two need each other right now, Reid," Fin cut in. "Both of you are in vulnerable positions, *placed* there, mind you, by the same enemy."

Reid held his cigar, leaning against the kitchen island, silent in the dim, smokey room.

Fin dipped his head low, shoulders slumping in relief as he saw Reid's gears turning over his words. He desperately needed to win him over.

"Now the king, I hear, told you the long of it —why they're here and such," Fin said, lifting his head. "I also hear you don't want to take them in as refugees unless they renounce their homeland and titles and become Redironers through and through. I understand the burden they would be placing upon your resources if they're allowed to stay under your protection in your borders, but King Waldock has offered to pay you handsomely for their supplies."

"You think I care about riches right now?" Reid rebutted, raising his voice. "Our people need *healing*, not *gold*. Their faith in law, in power, in leadership was just put through hell. I lead a broken people, Fin."

"And that's exactly what King Waldock's presence and cause offers. A chance for an actual recovery."

Reid was silent, but his expression had shifted. "Explain," he ordered.

Fin knew he had him. If Reid truly was a man that cared about the welfare of his people, he would be hard-pressed to overlook the prudence of what Fin was about to say.

"What your people just went through, it's going to happen again," Fin said, leaning in. "The White Cloaks have infiltrated the hierarchy of the Golden Crowns, the Black Steel kingdom, and Alumin, as they tried with Rediron. They're only getting bigger, more influential, more powerful. Those opposed to an oppressive cult's reign of terror, such as yourself, King Waldock, the Silver Crowns, and any others we can find, need to stand together and take swift action. We need to form a coalition between all free people, or the Crowned Kingdoms will fall to Umbraz."

Reid broke eye contact first, resting his eyes a

moment as he drew in another lungful of smoke, letting it out slowly before moving to take the seat next to Fin at the bar. He took the fresh glass of brandy and downed it in one go.

They sat there in the smoke and silence for some time. Fin knew the man had a weight upon his shoulders that few deserved to carry. He was sympathetic ...but that did not stop him from making sure the correct line of action was going to be taken.

Fin broke the silence. "Give your people a chance to recover from their persecutor. I know that right now, you want nothing more than to protect your people and get as much distance from the White Cloaks as you can, but sometimes the best recovery for a people is to allow *them* to right the wrongs done to them. Right now, there are a lot of people being wronged by Umbraz, not just Redironers. You could help instigate real justice for the people of this nation."

Reid rolled his thin cigar between his fingers, evening out the ember. After some thought, he admitted, "I suppose—there's some wisdom in what you're saying."

Fin nodded, relieved that they were seeing eye to eye. "I was hoping you'd say that. King Waldock seems honest enough a man—his son, Johnathan, too. They could be a boon to your flagging state. Who knows, with this union, it could mean the end to the Mad Queen's reign in the end. You could be building a long-term alliance if the Lost King and his son are reinstated after the war."

"'Who knows' and 'could bes' aren't worth a copper strip around these parts, Fin. Hope is a fool's game," Reid said as smoke leaked out from under his mustache. "Each time we've met, you've brought nothing but more burdens to my doorstep—like a dog bringing home a rotten carcass."

"Undue burden is the life of a king, Reid. Get used to it," Fin said and got up from the bar to leave.

"Fin," Reid called as Fin moved for the door. "Before you go, perhaps there's a subject you can shed some light on. You just might have more exposure to the ugly side of this Umbraz cult than most."

Setting his cigar in the tray, Reid moved into the den. He opened a side table drawer and withdrew a bundle of robes stained with dried blood.

"You recognize these?" Reid asked, bringing the bundle over to him.

"That damned priestess of Umbraz."

"Elise was her name," Reid confirmed. "This is what remains of her belongings. She's dead now; you made sure of that."

Reid handed over the robes to Fin to examine. "All other White Cloaks were driven out of the kingdom last week. Perhaps we should have held some for interrogation, but..." Reid paused, rubbing his stubble in thought. "The kingdom suffered enough hurt this last year. The people just wanted the White Cloaks gone. That's all we have left to try and piece together information about this cult. I was hoping that something in her possessions might spark—"

"*The Seam*," Fin whispered, eyes wide as he pulled out a string necklace of shimmering pearl-like objects.

"The Seam?" Reid asked, the phrase meaning nothing to him.

Fin didn't immediately answer, but his focus on the object told Reid that there was more to the pearl necklace than he had suspected.

"I might not have the answers to the full significance of this trinket, but I know of some that will."

CHAPTER 29 - REKINDLED BONDS

The next day, Reza awoke with the morning sun, feeling much better after the meal and restful evening she had with Cass. She moaned as she sat up in bed, rubbing her eyes when she saw someone sitting in the chair across from her.

"Fin?" she blurted out, seeing instantly that something was different about him.

He smiled to see her up and well, but it was a tired kind of smile—one that spoke of hidden troubles.

"Finally up, sleepy head? Sometimes I think you're half bear, hibernating like that as frequently as you do," he said, moving over to sit at her bedside.

She yawned, trying to shake off her tiredness. Fin shifted his tone and scolded, "You really should stop risking your life like you do. Thanks for bringing me back, but please, think of your health before you decide to perform another blessing."

"I'll heal whom I wish," she said.

"Girl…" Fin warned. He knew he'd not change her mind on the matter, but he was genuinely not happy with how reckless she had been on his behalf.

"Maybe next time I save your life, you could at least stay by my side till I awake." Her chilly reply was clearly in jest, but she could see the jab had taken Fin down a peg.

"Brutal," he moaned, running his hands through his hair.

Reza softened a bit. "You feeling okay? I was worried about the healing I gave you. Wasn't sure if I had finished the job before…"

"I'm fine," Fin replied, waving away her concern.

Reza placed a hand on Fin's leg, patting him to calm him. She could tell there was still something bothering him, more so than the healing and her quips.

"Fin, what's wrong?"

Fin sighed, feeling sleep-deprived exhaustion firmly set in. He took a small leather bundle out of the inner of his vest and handed it over to Reza.

"The priestess of Umbraz that I…*scotched* here weeks ago—she was carrying this," Fin said, pulling out the pearl necklace.

"My god," Reza breathed as she counted the number of prayer beads strung on the cord.

Her reaction piqued his interest. "You've seen something similar before?"

Reza nodded and leaned down to rummage through her gear at her bedside. Snatching a pouch from her things, she unstrung it and carefully pulled out a similar necklace, this one adorned with only a single pearl.

"Oh boy," Fin groaned, shaking his head, seeing now that whatever the religious symbols were, they were definitely important to the cult's ceremonies.

"Fin, do you know what these are?"

"They're tainted by the Seam; I know that. I've seen enough Seam residue to recognize that surreal pearlescent sheen. I figured Mal would know more about it. He's the expert on that realm."

"That...may be helpful, yes. Out of anyone we know, Malagar knows the most about the Seam. But... I think I know what they are, Fin. They're a conduit to Umbraz, or it to us," Reza said as she inspected both relics.

She had Fin's full attention now. "I had a vision back in Rosewood I've been meaning to talk with you about. I shared a vision with the Reverend Father and his Torchbearers. Within moments, we merged consciousness, and I saw what they saw. They worship an unrealized god—not yet fully developed. One that's from another time or place. They're not like the gods that we know of from the heavens or hells— Umbraz is from *another* place—perhaps the Seam is its birthing grounds. These pearls, I'm quite certain, are a link to him or maybe an anchor to our realm. Tethers that make his existence all the more real, and the more real he becomes to us, the more power he has in being able to interact and influence our realm."

"Are we in danger just by having them near us?" Fin asked.

"I'm...not sure. Perhaps Mal would know better the properties of the Seam," Reza speculated, looking at the pearls as though they would come alive at any moment. "But I have...tapped into its powers once. It is dangerous. I would advise to keep it covered, in a pouch. Don't touch the pearls themselves. I believe what they were able to do with your skull, they did so with the power of these pearls."

"Understood," Fin acknowledged, eyeing the stash of malevolent pearls. "We need Mal, Reza. Even with how bad off he was last time I saw him, he might be able to help."

"Not just Malagar. I need to consult with Lanereth and Terra," Reza said.

"Hmm," Fin considered, stroking his chin. "Might as well throw Cavok and Yozo in that list. We could use their muscle and skill. I could go; rush up and lead them here."

"No," Reza stated. "I'm no good with diplomacy. King Waldock seems like a stubborn man, and I don't know King Reid at all. I'd be useless here. You, on the other hand, know both men much better than me. Dare I say they seem to respect you."

"I suppose that makes the most sense, but..." Fin said, mulling over the reversal, "I worry about you on the road without company."

"You'll have to get used to sleeping without a bedmate again," Reza jived, nudging Fin with her shoulder.

He couldn't help but smile in spite of himself, nudging her back. "I don't know who you've been sharing a bed with, 'cuz bed*mate* would be the last way I'd describe our situation. More like bed*hog*." Her frown cracked, and he could see her struggling to hold back a giggle. "I'm serious, you thrash like crazy—and the bed's small enough as is. I haven't gotten a good night's sleep since we got here. Had to sleep on the damned floor two nights ago."

She swatted him hard on the arm. He relented and put the two pearl necklaces into the pouch. The mood turned somber as Fin handed it back to Reza for safe keeping.

"Guess you'll be needing these to show to Mal and Lanereth once you make it back to High Perch. Hopefully, they'll be able to tell you more about their importance."

She held the pouch in her hand a while. They both allowed the weight of what lay ahead of them to sink in for a moment before she set the pouch down on her pack. She knew she'd not be able to leave for High Cliffs for a few days yet. She was still weak. To be out on the open road on shaky legs, alone, was not a risk worth taking.

"It's morning, right?" she asked.

Caught slightly off guard, Fin nodded.

"Let's go see Sauvignon," she suggested. "I saw it from the roof last night. There's a market district close by. Maybe we could start there and grab some breakfast together somewhere in town."

"Reza Malay...I was not expecting that from you." Fin smirked, holding her hands in his. "Sure. Let's hit the town...but you're buying."

For all their tiffs and differences over the years, Fin had been a true companion to her. His words about their bond back in Alumin had stuck to her.

She smiled and squeezed his arm lovingly, thankful that he was by her side. She had never had family ties throughout her upbringing, other than perhaps Lanereth. She imagined that what she and Fin had was as close to a loving family bond as the genuine article.

CHAPTER 30 - THE SPELL OF REDIRON COUNTRY

"A round of Sauvignon ales, Anne," Reid said, kicking back in his chair, blowing smoke rings up over the table where Reza, Fin, and Johnathan sat. It was clear to the others that Reid was determined not to rush his usual visit to the Crow's Flight Tavern and had ordered a large serving of the tavern's famous bacon-wrapped venison tenderloins for the group.

Both Fin and Reza seemed comfortable enough, chit chatting with the others at the table. Fin even took Reid up on sharing a thin cigar with the newly crowned king, waxing on the quality of the leaf. All the while, however, Johnathan's typical rigid and direct mood seemed to temper what should have been an enjoyable atmosphere.

"A king that dines with his subjects," Johnathan remarked between a pause in conversation. "Quite unorthodox."

"Aye," Reid agreed at length after a long draw from his cigar.

"Needless exposure to the public. You're not

even accompanied by troops. If you wish your reign to last any length of time, you should be attended by Kingsguard, King Reid."

Reid took his time ruminating on the sentiment, holding his reply until after Anne placed down plates and a serving dish with the wrapped tenderloins.

"My man is over there at the bar talking with Ben," Reid said, his eyes directing the group to a man wearing a duster coat, who watched the group even as he spoke with the barkeep. "Morgan can handle any man in this city in a street fight. Besides, I'm not too bad with a sword myself. I'll be fine."

Johnathan eyed the king. Reid returned the man's determined gaze and took a sip of his fresh ale. "Besides, Rediron is more than a place to 'lord over' for me. This is *home*. And any man that tells me I can't *live* in it can go straight to the deep hells."

Johnathan nodded after a moment. "I suppose I can respect that. Tactically vulnerable, but...even a king cannot exhaust his whole life only tending to his duties."

"I'll smoke to that." Reid cracked the faintest hint of a smile as he took out a thin cigar and offered it to the warchief.

Johnathan accepted the gift and lit it on the table candle's flame, his face as stern as ever as he shared a few silent puffs with the former marshal.

"Reza," Reid puffed. "Fin told me about you heading back to Jeenyre. You sure you don't want an escort? I can send a Redironer with you."

"Or Cass. As I understand, she's been enjoying her time with you," Johnathan offered.

"No. Thank you both, but the horse you've given me is already more than enough," she said. "I feel much better after a few days' rest. I should be to High Cliffs Monastery within a week, no problem. Let's hope I can return with support to our shared cause."

"I'm sure Lanereth and Malagar will be willing to come to our aid. And make sure you lug Cavok along when you return. It's high time he sees the Crowned Kingdoms," Fin said. "With any luck, General Seldrin is successful in petitioning Silver Crowns officials to come and enter talks of an alliance with us—and that goes for Kaia with West Perch."

"Cheers to that," Johnathan said, holding up his ale. Everyone followed suit, clinking mugs.

The ale had been effective at loosening up both Reid and Johnathan after a pint. Everyone had ordered a meal after enjoying the side dish, and the mood lightened as Fin regaled them with stories and news from the Southern Sands. Reza reined him in from time to time, correcting him on embellishments along the way.

Lunch was scarcely done when Reza announced that she was going to hit the road before it got too late.

Saying her goodbyes to Reid and Johnathan, she and Fin made their way out to the post where their horses were hitched. After whispering some comforting words to her horse and soothing its mane, she turned to say her goodbyes to Fin. To her surprise, he was up on his horse, ready to head out.

"You're not staying with those two?" Reza asked, mounting her horse.

"I let them know that I was going to accompany you at least to Tarrolaine," Fin explained and started them on a walk down the busy street. Reza followed his lead.

They made their way out of the city without much chatter, heading out onto the open highway in a casual trot. The road was easygoing, and with only passing a few travelers and two Road Rangers, they spent most of the afternoon chatting up any subject that happened to tickle their fancy.

Before long, they were nearing Tarrolaine, and the sun began to ride low in the open country of Rediron, gracing the snow-capped peaks far in the distance. Though Fin had traveled that way a few times that year, it was Reza's first.

Her awe was transparent. Fin had rarely seen his companion so unguarded with her expressions of wonder as she let the cool mountain breeze rush across her features and through her locks.

"Out here in the open—it's so quiet." Her voice was naught but a whisper on the wind. "It's almost as if none of the world's problems even exist."

Fin smiled knowingly. In his travels, he had cherished the quiet times on the road the most. The long starry nights and grand vistas of the day on the open road had granted him the blessing of reflection, which he rarely got in the city. He had learned a lot about himself on the road that year.

"Rediron country tends to do that to ya, once you're out of the bustle of the streets and up in the mountains." Fin sighed, looking out over the endless wilderness along the Verdant Expanse to the south. "Who knows, one day I might hang up my daggers and settle down up here somewhere. I do fancy the place."

Reza was barely listening. Her horse came to a stop at the roadside to nibble on a full tuft of grass. She looked at peace, her eyes still closed as she took in the crisp mountain air.

Fin knew the world would soon be dark...but he waited there for her to soak in the warmth, wanting Reza to feel the last rays of sun on her face, untainted by the road ahead, before it faded into memory.

Thank you for being part of the adventure!

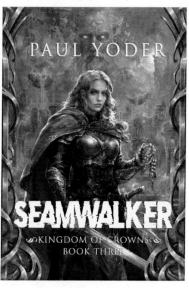

Seamwalker, book three in the **Kingdom of Crowns trilogy** is available on Amazon!

The birth of a new god is about to change the very fabric of reality. Reza and her crew are all that stand in the path of utter oblivion.

The saren knight Reza and her alliance of comrades rush headlong into the forces of Umbraz who has been amassing power and armies from the Golden Crown and the Black Steel kingdoms. The final battle draws near—death and chaos now reign supreme in the fury of war.

The zealots of Umbraz are determined to snuff out the lives of all those who intend to interfere with their god's summoning rite. It's a race against time as Umbraz approaches their reality and begins to emerge into the realm of Wanderlust.

Seamwalker is the concluding book in the thrilling fantasy Lands of Wanderlust saga, which puts captivating heroes against Lovecraftian horrors in the wonderfully detailed fantasy world of Una.

Visit me online for launch dates and other news at:

authorpaulyoder.com

tiktok.com/@authorpaulyoder

instagram.com/author_paul_yoder

amazon.com/stores/Paul-Yoder/author/B00D6NN4G0

goodreads.com/author/show/7096027.Paul_Yoder

Made in United States
North Haven, CT
31 October 2024

59672293R00178